TORRIE JONES

Dealing With The Outcast

First published by Amazon Publishing 2023

Copyright © 2023 by Torrie Jones

All rights reserved. No part of this publication may be reproduced, stored or transmitted in any form or by any means, electronic, mechanical, photocopying, recording, scanning, or otherwise without written permission from the publisher. It is illegal to copy this book, post it to a website, or distribute it by any other means without permission.

This novel is entirely a work of fiction. The names, characters and incidents portrayed in it are the work of the author's imagination. Any resemblance to actual persons, living or dead, events or localities is entirely coincidental.

Torrie Jones asserts the moral right to be identified as the author of this work.

First edition

*This book was professionally typeset on Reedsy.
Find out more at reedsy.com*

He didn't run away this time.

He ran towards what he believed in.

To my Eddie Munson and Heath Ledger/Patrick Verona fans, this one is for you.

Contents

Foreword	iii
Playlist	v
Jolie	1
Stevie	10
Jolie	15
Stevie	22
Jolie	30
Stevie	37
Jolie	40
Stevie	44
Jolie	51
Stevie	63
Jolie	69
Stevie	79
Jolie	85
Stevie	95
Jolie	101
Stevie	123
Jolie	134
Stevie	140
Jolie	151
Stevie	159
Epilogue	167
Afterword	174

About the Author 176
Also by Torrie Jones 178

Foreword

Authors Note:

Hello reader!

Please note that this book contains the following topics, but are not limited to:
Blackmail
Mentions of Suicide
Bullying
Anxiety
Mentions of Self Harm.

If this is something you can't read, I completely understand, please look after your mental health. That is what is most important.

Kinks mentioned in the book:
Choking
Mask Kink
Rough Sex

BDSM
Praise Kink
Again, if these topics are something you can't read about, I completely understand.

Playlist

Dealing With The Outcast - listen now on Amazon.

1. Master of Puppets - Metallica
2. Living On A Prayer - Bon Jovi
3. You Give Love A Bad Name - Bon Jovi
4. Always - Bon Jovi
5. If You Can't Hang - Sleeping With Sirens
6. Do It Now Remember It Later - Sleeping With Sirens
7. Every Breath You Take - The Police
8. Wings of a Dove - Madness
9. 10 Things I Hate About You - Leah Kate
10. you broke me first - Tate McRae
11. Ultraviolet - Stiff Dylans
12. She's So Lovely - Scouting For Girls
13. Sparks Fly (Taylor's Version) - Taylor Swift
14. Miss Americana & The Heartbreak Prince - Taylor Swift
15. Can't Help Falling in Love - Kina Grannis
16. Rock Me - One Direction

AND MORE!

Jolie

All fan fiction writers are horny people. What they're into varies, and it varies from odd, to past trauma, to needing attention, to God knows what else.

But everyone has their kinks. I would know.

Although, I wouldn't know. I'm a virgin. The virgin Mary, if you will. Or shall I say the Virgin Jolie as two of my friends call me.

Yet my mind has had sex over ten thousand times. I mean my characters. They've had sex in places that I'm jealous of and being put in positions a girl knows will be able to make her find some sort of release.

However, you can call me curious. Or, a very thorough romance writer, and avid reader. But so is everyone these days. With hashtags such as booktok, or bookstagram, books have taken over the world since the pandemic, and in the best way possible. It helps. Helps people's mental health, gets them more focused, and overall improves people's minds.

But if you were to tell your parents you're reading a book

about a guy and a girl and summed it up as an innocent romance, they wouldn't bat and eye. But if you were to tell them you were reading a book that has more red flags than the average man and how you've fell in love with a fictional character that will never exist cause men in this day and age are lazy and don't know what they want, they would probably send you to a nut house. So, you sum it up as an innocent romance, yet imagine you were the one being choked.

Currently my two characters are going at it for the second time in this what I would like to say is my first novel, but then I would tell a lie. This is draft twenty-something. I just can't seem to get it right.

Daniel and India. He's her neighbor's brother. He's grumpy, a firefighter, rude and she's a ray of sunshine. The classic trope everyone falls for.

He's a bad guy. *Swoon...*

He gets into bar fights. He's a family man and he protects his own. He had a girlfriend, until they had a very public break up in the street and India had to grab her popcorn. She was ecstatic, because finally he's single and she might be able to shoot her shot. But he shot first. I mean he shot a load after he watched her pleasure herself through her bedroom window. They watched themselves and it was the most erotic feeling in the world. One of many things she liked. Being watched. *Ugh same.* I sometimes feel jealous of my characters, because they're having fun while I'm writing their fun, still a virgin and waiting for a man to so much as touch me.

I've not even had my first kiss. Yet if you see the boys in this small town you would understand. Mommy's boys, who barely get by most of them want to be doctors, teachers, personal trainers. I just want a man who's going to treat me like a princess in pubic, but a freak in the sheets is that so much to ask?!

Ugh it is, but hopefully, when I go to college in the summer, I might be able to find someone who will be able to make me feel euphoric. Deep down I doubt it, but a girl has got to dream.

I've still got to get through my exams first, it's only February, and I have so much studying to do, but I'm currently writing another sex scene instead of studying for my history test on Friday.

There is a slight knock at my door, and I quickly move my papers out of the way that have doodles of hands cupping breasts and God knows what else.

My Mom opens the door. "Hey Jolie-bear, you gonna get some sleep?" She asks leaning in on the door. I'm legally eighteen, yet sometimes she still treats me like a child.

"Yeah, just doing some last-minute studying." I say with smile. I'm studying alright, how two people can fuck each other senseless twice in one night. I look at my mom, and I might as well be her doppelganger. Apart from her now having blonde hair, we aren't that much different looking. Same height, same weight. Sometimes people ask if we're sisters.

"Okay, well not much later, you have school in the morning." She reminds me.

"I know, Mom." I express. "Ten more minutes." I say and she nods before wishing me goodnight and shutting the door.

I'm pleased she leaves me to do what I need to. I keep my business very private but give them enough information, so they don't get suspicious. Last thing I need to do is give my family a heart attack over the novel I'm writing. However, if I even decide to publish anything, it will be under a pen name. Evangeline Lloyd. No where near to my name that my family would work out it's me.

Honestly don't think I would ever be able to explain myself. Because how do you explain to your family you create characters nowhere near to yourself who have sex more times than they eat and have kinks that you dream of? I think I would end up killing them.

I do as I promise, I hide my sins in my locked box and put the key back around my neck. I keep it close, because my dirtiest, darkest secrets in there, and the last thing I need is for anyone to find that out.

Making sure I have everything packed for school, I practically jump back into bed. It's warm in this house, but I was nicely tucked under the covers, and I crave that warmth again. I begin to get comfortable in the hopes tonight, my mind doesn't go wild, and I start to think of new scenarios to put my characters in, because they've really been put through the ringer.

* * *

I run out of the door and to my car. I'm not late by any means, but I do like to get there early so I can avoid bumping into the school bully's or being a target.

The whole school fears them, but they are the classic mean girl and boy, cheerleader and jock. You get the gist.

The drive to school is boring but quick, but I can't say I'm surprised. I am making good time today which means I won't have to deal with them.

In summary, if you're late, and you interrupt their scour through the hall, they will publicly shame you. You would probably be best just hiding outside, but just as much as the

Jolie

students are afraid of them, so are the teachers.

They have so much power, probably too much power. And it's frightening how much they get away with. All the students were hoping that when the new headteacher joined in the summer last year, that he would make changes, turns out he's on their payroll and doesn't do anything to stop them.

I head into the school clutching onto my backpack as I head towards my locker to retrieve my notebook for first period. I like to make myself invisible and not draw to much attention to myself. Today, I'm wearing a dark sage green jumper, black jeans, and black boots. Basic. But until I leave this hell hole, I won't be able to wear anything that I want to wear. Cowboy boots and cute summer dresses, but in this town? Around them? Ha!, you'll have to get approval. "Did you hear?" My excited best friend, Lauren practically runs to me to say down the corridor.

"Heard what?" I laugh as she links my arm.

"He's back!" She whispers, but it wasn't much of a whisper, I reckon the janitor down the corridor heard her.

"I have no idea who you're referring to." I say stopping in my tracks. I try not to get involved in any gossip, especially in a school that's full of it. Bullying can cause depression, and depression can cause suicide in some cases, and in this school its brutal.

"Stevie Pritchard." Lauren says, hoping to get some reaction.

"So?" I say, linking her arm and dragging her towards our lockers that are right beside each other.

"Don't you remember?" She says lightly shoving me. "He went to jail for four months for assaulting that police officer." She explains, and as much as I appreciate the recap, I remember it well.

Dealing With The Outcast

It was the school dance, and Stevie the freak, as the popular kids call him, got too drunk at the winter formal and punched a security guard. Not a police officer, he would have been sent out of state for that, but he did it local, served four months, and got out, well; today apparently.

Stevie is loud, weird, and obnoxious. Freak is harsh word; I would call him more of an outcast than anything. He doesn't belong to one group, he's a little bit of a loner, like me. He does have one friend, which sometimes keeps him in check, but also sometimes joins in on the chaos. They belong together, and one day they'll end up in jail together.

Everyone knows that Stevie is bad news. He doesn't listen to the rules, he's in a band and he's every mother's worst nightmare. Tattoos of Anime, song lyrics and stupid things like the chicken from Moana.

His parents pretty much just gave up on him, if he graduates, it will honestly be a miracle. Yet no one is expecting him to do that.

You can hear everyone talking about it, how one of the jocks heard from his dad that Stevie got out and he's back in school today. He's just bad news and the more I avoid him, the better my life is.

I don't think Stevie and I have had a proper conversation; I think in total I might have spoken two words to him in the entire time I've been here.

People begin lining the halls, because we all know at any second the popular kids will begin gracing our presence with their fake boobs, fake teeth, and fake attitude.

And like clockwork, they arrive. Matilda George and Brandon Pogue. The head cheerleader and the jock, and the meanest kids in school. Following them is their minions, Dior

Jolie

(yes like the brand), Elle (named after Elle Woods as her parents want her to go to college to be a lawyer, doubtful if she keeps getting stopped for possession.) Brandon's group of friends Justin and Ethan.

They walk almost in slow motion while the others follow elegantly behind. You can stare, but not for too long. With the way they act, I honestly feel they believe themselves to be royalty, when in fact, they are cowards, bullies.

In the middle of their announcement to the school, the door slams behind them, and the whole corridor jumps.

And there he stands, making a grand entrance as always, is Stevie Pritchard. Lead singer of Death Due, a rock bad including Stevie on guitar and backing vocals, his friend keyboard on drums, Esther White on drums and for vocals, Sam Oswald. An older kid, the original outcast.

"What do you think you're doing?" Matilda snaps, moving past her minions in a rage as she stares at Stevie, who is grinning like a maniac.

"Oh, I'm sorry..." His dark, husky voice says with humor. "Did I ruin your moment?" He grins.

"Aren't you supposed to be in jail?" Matilda snaps back, which only makes the grin on Stevie's face grow wider.

"Just got out, did all of you miss me?" He playfully pouts. He's changed, although that's not surprising. He has more tattoos now; his hair is longer, and it looks like he might have permed it. Odd, but not odd enough when you know the lengths this man will go to just to not fit in.

"Ew, no." Matilda says in disgust. That only makes Stevie laugh.

"Come on now, Tilly," he taunts her, "I know you've missed me." he speaks. "In fact, I know you've all missed me." He says pointing around and looking around at his peers. "But in case anyone has forgotten who I am, I'm Stevie Pritchard." He says taking a bow. "But you might know me as Stevie the freak."

"The name still sticks." Ethan snaps to Stevie, who nods with a psychotic grin.

"And it seems that you have been walking these halls like you own them—" Stevie begins, and Ethan begins to interrupt but he stops him. "So, that's gonna come to a stop."

Brandon and Matilda laugh. "So, what, you run these halls now?"

Stevie continues to smile. "Of course, Tilly. Because I'm here to prove that no matter who your parents are, we're all gonna end up the same. Well, at least us hard working kids will. You will just keep getting things handed to you. And that doesn't sound fun. You need to live a little."

His speech catches Matilda off guard, cause he's right. She's daddy's princess.

He walks closer and leans in her ear. "You'll amount to nothing; you'll be some slut who ends up getting pregnant with the wrong guy. Then you will see how the real people live."

He walks away from her. No one calls Matilda a name and gets away with it. But he doesn't care. Stevie lives for the thrill, he's kind of narcissistic, yet his actions remind me of Robin Hood. Wanting to do right by the people so the rich don't succeed.

As he walks by me, we lock eyes, and even though he smiles at me, and I know it's not to me; but I suddenly feel butterflies in my stomach.

I shake it off. Although Stevie, if he didn't look like an eighty's rocker, is a good-looking guy. I have standards and dreams I wanna uphold, and a life with Stevie Pritchard would mean that you'd always be in trouble.

Stevie

They enrage me, infuriate me with how they think because their parents pay a substantial amount of money to the school, that they have the right to treat anyone the way they do. No one should be in fear because of some preppy teenagers.

If I didn't exist, the people of this school would fear them, just like they have for the last four months while I've been in jail. It was the most boring time of my life, living by the rules, being beat up. I'll never go back there again.

It is only because the police officer I got in the altercation with was one of the minion's dads. If it had been anyone else, a simple apology, possibly some community service and I wouldn't have missed out on so much, which meant they could get away with making a mockery of the school.

Lining the halls so people can worship you should be some kind of need to have a cult. They crave the attention; they need it to survive. *BLAHHH.*

How they think it's normal like something you would see

on a TV show, proves how delusional they are, as well as my fellow peers for not laughing in their faces. I don't doubt by the end of the week I will have had my head down the toilet, I'll go home with a black eye and probably a few broken ribs. After all, they have a reputation to uphold. And I only wish to demolish it.

After collecting my schedule from the office, I head to my first class of the day, Math. The worst kind of subject and even worse when you're me and you don't really need it. I'm not that dumb that I don't know how to count or do simple equations. I might need simple math in the future, but I doubt I'll ever need to learn about angles and shapes.

"Mr. Pritchard, nice to see you again." Mr. Franks greets me as I enter his class. He's mid-forties, a bit of a smart-ass. Which is why I like him.

"All the better for seeing you, sir." I say with a grin as I take my seat at the back. I may not have been here for the past few months, but this is my seat, and It has been since the start of the school year.

"I'm going to assume you have brought at least a pen with you today, Stevie?" He asks, looking at me through his eyelashes. Reaching into my pocket, I pull out exactly that, a pen. Usually, I would just let the teacher give me one, but let's just say that at least for today, I'm trying to be a better person. "Fantastic. Okay, class…" Mr. Franks begins, and I immediately know that for the next hour, I'm going to hate every second of this class, because it is probably something I have learned already.

By the time that this class is over, I practically jump out of my seat and head for the door, just wanting to get today over with as soon as possible. "Mr. Pritchard." I hear him summon as I'm practically through the door. "A moment please?"

I want to groan, but instead, I listen and push through my peers as I head towards the front of his desk. "How can I help?" I ask smugly.

He ignores the smile. "Stevie, before you returned to school, the jail had asked you to complete a test, yes?" He asks, to which I nod in response. "Well, Stevie, you failed. All of them. All classes."

I feel my face fall ever so slightly. "What?"

"I'm sorry, Stevie. But they ran it through two different people, you failed."

I almost want to laugh. "So, what does that mean?" I ask him, placing my hands behind my back.

"Well, if you don't get your grades up, you're going to fail your entire high school year. Meaning you may have to stay here another year until you pass."

That makes me laugh. I could just drop out; I know deep down that the people who checked my answer on that stupid test only failed me because they knew how much trouble it would cause me on the outside. And staying in this hell hole for another year isn't possible. I would rather off myself, than be stuck here.

"With all due respect, Mr. Franks, I don't need a lot of the subjects I am currently studying, I only do it to make my parents happy—"

"And how would they feel if they found out that you failed your back-to-school test from jail?" He cuts me off. *They'd be furious, yet not surprised.*

"They wouldn't be best pleased. But like I've told them before, it's my life. I choose how I live it."

He takes a long exhale, looking at me with disappointment. "Stevie," he begins, standing out of his chair. "You're a smart kid, if you use your brain." I frown, wanting to argue with him. "But your head is so far in the clouds that you need to remember that school is a way for you to make a name for yourself."

I smile at him. "School isn't just what you need to succeed in life, Mr. Franks."

He exhales again. "No. But it's a start." he explains. *Fair point.* "Look," he says as he stands in front of me at his desk. "I'm giving you a month to make some changes. That means you need to get a tutor. I'm giving you the option as a human being, without telling your parents. But eventually if I don't see any progress, I will be informing your parents, and you will fail this entire year and you'll be forced to join in the next year. No band. No tour. Nothing. Do you understand?" He says this time with more force.

I smile, hinting that I understand him. "Crystal."

After leaving Mr. Franks office with no intention of getting a tutor one bit, I head slowly to my next lesson. "Oi! Freak!" I hear someone shout before my head is slammed into the lockers at the end of the hall. "Think you're funny, huh?" Brandon slams me against the lockers again.

"Depends on who you ask." I grin, looking up at him. That only seems to make him angrier as he kicks me to the floor. I'm taller than Brandon, and since going to prison I've gained some muscle. Not a lot, but enough to show this punk who he's messing with. I will one day. I'll get him back.

"Pull another stunt like that, freak, and you'll end up where you belong." He grins at me, and I can very lightly smell the breakfast he had this morning. Eggs. Wonderful. After slamming me in the locker once more, Brandon and his little band of friends' head towards the gym.

People pass me by, not offering to check on me or offer any assistance. But that is normal here. You don't want to be associated with me. I'm Stevie the freak. Or at least that's what everyone calls me.

Jolie

After arriving back home, I quickly avoid my parents. It's soon going to be the anniversary of my brother, Isaac's death. And when this time of year comes around, they are unbearable to be around. And I say that in the sweetest way possible.

They want to do lots of things that he would have enjoyed. Such as go to a concert, go to his favorite place to eat, drink his favorite drinks, the list is endless. The issue I have is that we have to spend a full week mourning once again. It's like our entire lives have to revolve around this entire week. Because the rest of the year, my parents only speak to me when they feel as though they are doing their duties as a parent. Other than that I'm invisible.

After Isaac died, photos that were once of the both of us, changed to just him. Like the whole house is a shrine to him. I think there might be a picture of me on the wall in the kitchen, but I'm in the background and of course, Isaac is front and center.

I don't hate them for it, I just don't really know how they feel. I know I'm sad because I lost my brother, but I can't even imagine how they feel. They lost a son - a child. The pain is unbearable.

"Jolie bear?" I hear my mom call after me. "Can you come here?"

I sigh but do as I'm told. She must have heard me shut the door. I head in the direction of the kitchen, where she and my dad are sat at the breakfast bar, giving me a small smile.

"How was school?" Dad asks.

"Okay. Nothing happened really." I say as I place my bag down on the floor, and lean on the counter. "So…" I say looking around the kitchen. "What's up?"

They exchange a look between each other. "Well Jolie, you know how it is Isaac's birthday next month?" Mom asks me. I nod, not wanting to say what was really on my mind. "Well, we are thinking of starting this week with the celebrations. It will be good since it would have been his twenty-first birthday."

I want to take a long deep sigh and give them both a hug. Since Isaac died, remembering him is the only thing that keeps them going. In some cases, some would say they are delusional. Sometimes, I think they still believe he is alive, walking around somewhere.

"That sounds good." I say with a smile, before picking up my bag from the floor. "I have homework, but that does sound good. He would have loved that."

I make my way up the stairs, pleased to get out of that situation and into my own space. After shutting the bedroom door, I lock it, just in case they decide to want to carry on the conversation.

I practically run to my bed. Although school wasn't terrible,

Jolie

it wasn't great. Even worse now Stevie Pritchard is back in school.

He finds any and every way to make people feel uncomfortable, but as long as you don't associate with him, your life will be worth living.

I do find him brave for calling out Matilda and Brandon. No one would have dreamed to stand up to them, everyone is too afraid. There were rumors that the reason Stevie was sentenced was actually based on a lie, but then again that also could have been untruthful. Stevie gets in all sorts of trouble; he would be the kind of guy if I brought him home to my parents they would find any and every reason to have me committed to some sort of asylum.

After emptying my bag and placing books and other things on my desk, I get a start on my homework. Exam season will be starting soon, and I really need to get a focus on my studies. I'm a straight A student, however, I want nothing more than to pass my exams and be done with this school and head to college.

And although I find myself needing to do my homework, my heart is saying spend a hour or so on my novel. I'm really deep into the middle part of the story, where India and Daniel are doing fun things such as date nights and shower sex, something I, a girl who has spent too much time on fan fiction websites, would know something about mentally, just not physically.

I decide to listen to my heart and for the next hour of my evening, I spend it devoted to the raunchy sex scene, or should I say one of many.

Sex is something I know so much about, but have no experience in. When you read about kinks and fantasies in stories or online, you would normally cringe at the thought of it, but when you're immersed in telling a story, you almost get a horny glaze over everything as you write and you find yourself either feeling turned on or jealous, because if you're like me, you're the fucking virgin Jolie.

When it happens, I want it to be special. Memorable? Probably not as it will be awkward, but I want it to be something like what you read in books. Movies I can't relate to, as sometimes you can tell the chemistry is fake. And that's not what I want, I want it to be meaningful.

I've heard nightmares from girls who had sex and it lasted only forty seconds, or that the guy who talked a big game, had the tiniest dick that it could pass as a grain of rice. It happens, and in all honesty, I just hope it doesn't happen to me.

Last thing I want is to be embarrassed over the fact I either moan weirdly or that the guy who I decide is a good fit at the time, can't even locate the clit and decides to fuck the sofa. It's happened, I've heard horror stories.

After my wild hour of character sex and becoming jealous of them, I feel my stomach grumble. Although I'm hungry, the thought of actually socializing with my parents, who will only stick to the one topic for a twenty-minute sit down, will drive me insane, and for a few minutes I debate starving myself. But suddenly I remember that food is love and food is life, and I can last twenty minutes if it means I get a meal and I will be able to focus while doing my homework.

I place my notes, scribbles and words of a deranged sex pest away from any sight of my parents as I unlock my bedroom door and head down the stairs.

The delicious smell of salmon fills my nostrils, and as I eagerly approach the kitchen, I can see that I'm just in time as Mom is plating things up to bring to the table. "Jolie, can you set

Jolie

the table please? Dinner will be one minute." She announces, and I do as I'm told without saying a word. Remembering to set a place for Isaac next to Mom. Something I do every day.

"I hope you're hungry." Dad says as he approaches from the hall. "Salmon, rice and veggies." He says as he begins to bring over a few of the dishes to the table.

"Sounds good." I smile as I bring the last remaining dish and the water that Mom placed on the counter next to it for me.

"So," Mom begins as she begins to plate what would have been Isaac's food. "I think we should start looking into activities to do, to celebrate Isaac's death." She begins, barely breaking eye contact.

"Great idea, darling." Dad says with a smile. "Any ideas?" He turns to me, but I suddenly feel my mind go blank as every single idea leaves my brain.

"He always wanted to go surfing, maybe we can take a trip and do that this year?" Mom suggests, that brings me out of the dark hole.

"Fantastic!" Dad exclaims. "You up for a trip, Jolie bear?" He asks as I shove some food in my mouth, not wanting to entertain this conversation but knowing I have to. I finish the food in my mouth and hesitate for a moment.

"I have tons of exams coming up, and I really want to just get through my final year of high school before I head off to college, I don't really want to take any time off." I explain as softly as I can.

They exchange a look. "College?" Mom asks almost in disbelief. "Who said you were going off to college?"

I stare at her. *Is she serious?* "Mom, I'm going to college next fall. I've already started applying." I remind her. This isn't the first time she's heard about this; she knows I don't want to stay in our tiny little town.

"I thought you were just going to find a job here. You don't need college, darling. It won't benefit you." She says before taking a bite out of her salmon.

I look to my dad for help, but he is avoiding my eyes at all costs. "I don't know who told you that, but it certainly wasn't me, Mom." I say, slightly raising my voice.

"Jolie," She begins, taking yet another bite of salmon, this time it's paired with some veggies. "We won't be paying for college, because you don't need it. You just need to stay here, where you can get a little job and find a nice husband and live with us." She says as if it's the most normal thing in the world.

Her level of delusion has reached an all-time high, but instead of causing a scene, I pick up my plate, this time, my father manages to look me in the eyes. "I'm eating my dinner in my room, I have homework." I say, picking up my water and heading straight down the hall, ignoring my mother's pleas to come back to the table.

I lock my door and take a seat at my desk, staring at my dinner now feeling repulsed after the conversation that has just went on downstairs.

I'm not completely heartless when I say that I understand how she's feeling. With me wanting to go off to college, I dread to think of how much anxiety that brings her knowing another child will be leaving the home and moving away for school. But she can't expect me to be locked up in this house like Belle from Beauty and The Beast. I have my own life to live, and staying here in this house isn't part of my plan.

The more she tries to keep me locked away, the more I will resent her in the future, and I don't want that to happen. But unless something changes, it will end that way.

Jolie

Sometimes, I wish I had a hobby. Because anything right now would be better than staying in the house with my parents.

Stevie

Band practice went off without a hitch.

It was great to be around my friends again, and back to playing my music.

That was the only thing that got me by while I was in jail. Music. Some of the people on my block were allowed CD players. So sometimes we got to listen to some cool music. It was good, but I don't think I could have classed any of the people on my block friends, they were more like people who understood me, who two just wanted to get out and back to their lives.

"So, Stevie," My band mate, Sam asks me as we finish practice. "Were you anyone's bitch?" He laughs, as does the rest of the band.

"Very funny, Sam." I mock, placing my guitar back in its bag. "But no, I didn't become anyone's bitch."

"Damn." He teases. "You would have made a pretty bitch."

The whole group laughed, even me. "So, how did you guys manage without me?" I ask.

Stevie

"Oh, you know..." Esther jokes, "quite well actually." She smiles at me.

Esther and I have always had a on-and-off thing... but recently she found a older boy a town over and they've been dating for the past three months. I mean good for her, but I kind of miss our time together. Not like I'd have a relationship with her... the woman is more unhinged than I am and that is saying something.

Sam's phone begins to ring, and as he stares at the number, almost in disbelief, the rest of us eagerly tell him to take the call. "Answer it, Sam!" I shout, trying to get him to click the screen.

After another second, he does so, and I've never heard someone shake while they speak before. "H-hello?" He stutters.

His eyes widen as he listens carefully to whatever the other person is saying on the other end. Esther, Donny and I all stare, watching and waiting to see if he will tell us who it is, or if he'll breathe, cause for the last minute or so; I don't think I've seen him take a breath. "Oh my god that's amazing!" He exclaims almost jumping up and down like an excited child on Christmas. "Great! Yeah! Okay, yeah. Okay, yeah. Okay I'll tell them. Goodbye." He says on repeat before looking at us all. Defending You Forever have asked us to be their supporting act for their American tour!" He exclaims and I feel my soul leave my body.

Defending You Forever are the first punk-rock band that made me fall in love with music and the reason I want to be a musician. They are the reason we all started this band, why we do covers of their songs, and write our own music almost as a dedication. "Are you actually being serious?" Donny asks, grabbing Sam by the arm tight, almost as if he's pulling him down from the clouds.

"That was their manager. He said that JD seen the music video to our song blinded and asked that we be the supporting act in the summer next year!" He exclaims to all of us.

None of us can believe it, but at the same time; we are all screaming with excitement. This is a huge deal for all of us. Defending You Forever is the reason we all became musicians. And being able to do a tour with them would be not only the best thing to ever happen in our lives but also it would be the greatest honor.

After celebrating with a couple of beers at Sam's place after band practice. I begin to head home. Although my parents know I'm in a band, and where I would be. I don't really feel like talking to them right now about it.

Since getting back from jail, they have been on my case about every little thing. They only agreed to the band practice, so I wouldn't start trouble; yet I'm never the one that starts it; it's normally someone else I just join in on the chaos.

I stand on the trash can, place my guitar on the top of the garage roof and step up, heading towards my bedroom window. It's not late by any means, it's barely eight o'clock; but I was told to be back by six-thirty and since celebrating the new and up and coming potential tour with my favorite band, I've went a tiny bit over schedule.

I sneak into my bedroom, ducking my head as I head through the window. And as I stand, I am greeted with the most furious faces of my parents. "Crap." I say out loud.

"Language, young man!" Mom exclaims.

"Stevie, come on. We told you eight." Dad whines to me as I head towards my bed.

"Yeah, I know…" I begin to whine as I face plant my bed.

Stevie

"And you've been drinking!" Mom exclaims. I raise my head from the pillow to look at her.

"I had two." I say in my defense.

"Unbelievable..."

"Why, Stevie?" Dad asks. "You promised your parole officer you were going to do better!"

I frown my brows. "And I am!" I rise to meet him. "The band got offered to tour next year with Defending You Forever."

My parents stare blankly at me. "What?" They almost say in unison.

"The band got offered to open up for my favorite band. It's the opportunity of a lifetime!"

Dad stares at me, almost as if he didn't believe the words coming out of my mouth.

"Stevie... you can't." Mom says and I divert my eyes to her.

"What?"

"Stevie, you're not going on tour."

"What!"

"You heard me!" She shouts. My Mom never raises her voice to me. Not like she just did. "Your grades are in shambles; you're going to amount to nothing." She says harshly which completely takes the breath out of my lungs.

Mom has never been one to support my music, it's always been my dad. He bought me all of my favorite CDs growing up, he bought me my guitar, took me to concerts, came to see my band play. Mom has never really come to any of them. Mainly because she doesn't like the music.

"Candice, I think that is a bit much, Hun..."

"No, John. It's not. You've encouraged this behavior from the start. It needs to stop now." She says, moving closer to me. "Get your grades up, Stevie. Then it's off to community college for you." She glares at me before leaving my bedroom and slamming the door, leaving both me and my dad stunned at her outburst.

"Look, son. I'll talk to her when she calms down." Dad reassures me while placing his hand on my shoulder. "I'm proud of you son." He says, before leaving the room.

He's never been one to let me give up on my dreams, so I doubt he will start now. They always talk about happy wife, happy life. But when it comes to my mom, she's normally great, until I went to jail. She worried herself sick while I was in there and she really didn't have a reason to worry.

I was surrounded by nineteen other kids who had all been placed in here for bigger things like me, such as drug possession and assault. But they were all kids, all of us. I ended up spending my birthday in jail, which sucked. But Mom still requested that she bring cake and fake candles so she could sing happy birthday.

Deep down, I know she knows I didn't do anything wrong that night. Hell, I know I didn't do anything wrong that night. But thanks to Brandon and his dad… I ended up in jail for four months. Some would say I'm a push over. I just let them do what they want and beat me up the way that they want cause it's easier. But if I fight back, I'll end up in jail. God forbid in this town you defend yourself.

Brandon and his dad have too much power. But then so does Matilda George and her family. Their ancestors built this town from the ground up and have one of the wealthiest businesses in this part of the area. Real Estate is the way forward! Or at least that is what the hundreds of billboards around town say. Her father, Hunter George's face everywhere.

Pulling my guitar out of my bag, I launch myself over to my

Stevie

bed and begin to play very light notes from Defending You Forever's new song, til' death. I'm not hungry as I decide that being told that I'll amount to nothing by my mom is all the fuel I need for this evening.

* * *

The next morning, I decide that leaving through the window isn't probably the best idea, and besides, I'm starving. I decide the face my mom head on.

Dad would have calmed her down by now. And maybe, if I was lucky, he would have told her to come to her senses.

As I reach the bottom of the stairs, I spot my mom and dad sit at the kitchen table, enjoying a cup of what smells to be coffee. "Morning." I mutter and head in the direction of the fridge.

"There is food on the side for you, I just plated it up." Mom says, and as I turn, I notice the plate of food waiting for me. Waffles and syrup.

"Thank you." I say with a small smile as I take the plate and head towards the table.

The air is so thick with tension, you can cut it with a knife. I eagerly eat my breakfast. Mom's waffles are the best since she makes them from scratch.

"Stevie," She stops me as I'm about to take another bite. I direct my eyes to her and place my fork down on the plate. "I think we should talk about last night." She expresses, and with a quick glance at my dad, I give her my full attention.

"I was unfair on you last night." She admits. "I was selfish, and angry and it all comes back to the fact that we lost you for four months, Stevie."

She begins to become tearful, which I hate. I despise the fact that for four months, I put my family through the worst pain in their lives and I was gone for so long.

"The thought of you leaving this time for a tour," she trails off, wiping her tears for a moment. "It sent me over the edge, and I said somethings I didn't mean."

"It's okay." I reassure her, but she places her hand up to stop me from saying anything more.

"It isn't Stevie. I'm sorry." She apologizes and I give her a weak smile, hinting that I forgive her. "Anyway, I want you to know that I'm not completely heartless, and after your father's convincing-" She glances to him, and he gives her a goofy smile. "We have agreed to let you go on the tour."

I pushed my chair back and stare at her, my head in my hands. "Are you serious?" I ask them, to which they both nod. I almost leap over the table to hug them both. "Thank you! Thank you!" I repeat which causes my mom to laugh.

"Stevie, there are conditions." She expresses and I feel my heart stop. Shit, of course there are conditions. I stand beside her, waiting for her to list them. "We know about the test you failed in jail." She says and I feel all of my excitement just dwindling away. "So, as long as you get a tutor, you study as much as you can, and you pass your end of year exam; you can go on the tour."

I stare at her. A tutor? Unless she hires someone from a town over, no one is going to tutor me. "That's going to be difficult." I express honestly and her browns frown.

"How?"

"Because I'm the local freak, Mom. No one will want to tutor me."

She gives me a face. "Of course, they will Stevie, you have

plenty of friends."

I stare at my dad for some sort of support. "Candice, I think we should just hire a tutor…" He expresses for me.

"Shush, John. Stevie, ask one of your peers. You have until the end of the week to have a tutor." It's Wednesday. How the hell am I meant to convince some nerd to tutor me before Friday? I might as well accept my fate that I won't be going on this tour, but as long as I please my mom with the idea that I at least tried, she may hire someone to tutor me.

Jolie

After a very short drive to school, I decide to just head straight to my first class. I avoided my parents this morning and said I had a meeting about potentially joining a after school club, which was a lie.

They would want to talk about this trip they are planning, and although my brother would have loved it, I really want to just focus on my life and stop having them dictate everything in my life.

My Mom being so delusional to think I would stay here to please her and have my dreams crushed is ridiculous. I'm going to college, and if I have to get a loan to do so, I will. She gave her dreams to have two kids, and although I'm grateful; I don't feel like following in her footsteps.

School is busy today, the jocks are getting ready for a game next week so there are lots of things to do if you're on the committee, that just doesn't include me. Posters and banners line the walls and I feel as though I'm in a High School Musical movie and Troy Bolton is about to start singing What Time Is

Jolie

It? down the hall, and every break off into song and dance.

Living in a small town, almost everyone knows everyone, which is why when you do something wrong, your family is sometimes shamed for it. Which is incredibly unfair.

When Isaac died, there was some awful rumors created by some of the wealthier people in this town. Rumors I don't care to retell but let's just say they were both obnoxious and disgusting to Isaac's nature. Besides, these people never knew him the way we did. I was barely sixteen when he died, yet it had such an impact on our family that people were afraid to talk to us when we did leave the house.

But when Lauren moved to town, she didn't have a clue what had been going on and saw another lonely girl like herself who was in need of a friend. And ever since we have been joined at the hip.

As I approach my locker, she waits for me, eagerly handing me a piece of paper before I put in my combination. Her long golden locks are curled today, and her colorful cardigan and Mom jeans match her aesthetic. Edgy.

"What's this?" I ask her as I read it over. It's a request for a tutor. For Stevie Pritchard. "Why are you giving me this?"

"Because you are one of the smartest girls in school." She explains, giving me the look as if I should agree. "Besides, you need to leave that awful job of yours."

I sigh. She hates the fact I work at the busiest local pizza spot in town. "Funny. But no." I say handing her the piece of paper back.

"Jolie, it's paid, it's two nights a week and if you accept it, you might get some sort of street cred…"

"Or lose anything that I did have to be known at the shy girl who tutored Stevie Pritchard. No thank you. I wish to remain invisible."

She sighs. "Suit yourself, but it will be a matter of time before he comes to find you himself." She says slightly walking away.

"He would have to know who I am first!" I call after her. She laughs but continues to head towards her first class. I grab my first book of the day out of my locker and place some other bits in there too. Things that I won't need till later.

As I shut my locker door, I am greeted with the smiling face of Stevie Pritchard, leaning against my locker. "Hi." He greets me. I turn to walk away, but he catches up to stand in front of me. "Come on, Jolie. Don't be so rude."

"What do you want Stevie?" I ask bluntly. The fact he is standing so close to me is making me uncomfortable. And I hate to be like the other kids in the school that just ignore him, but I like to remain as invisible as possible.

"I'll cut to the chase," he begins, placing his hand on the locker as he towers over me, his cologne filling my nostrils as if he is trying to drug me with his bad boy scent and the mix of tobacco. Stevie smokes. An awful habit that he, and a few of the other kids in this town have. "I'm in need of a tutor. And word on the street is that you're a smart cookie." He gleams at me. There are barely any kids in the hallway now as they have all headed off to their classes.

"I'm sorry, Stevie. I can't tutor you." I say as I begin to walk away from him, but I feel him grab my arm and pull me into a cupboard. "Stevie what the hell!" I shout at him.

"Be truthful with me, Jolie." He demands. "Are you refusing to tutor me because you're embarrassed to be seen with me?" He asks.

I'm never one to hurt people's feelings, but being this close to Stevie is making me a little uncomfortable. "I'll be honest,

Jolie

you dragging me into the janitor's closest wasn't on my yearly bingo card. I stay out of the way. I'm a ghost and if I'm honest I've mastered it. But you, Stevie, are the loudest, most obnoxious guy I have ever met, and you put your needs in front of everyone else so you have something to gain. So yes, I am embarrassed to be seen with you. Not because I am embarrassed of you, I couldn't care less about you; but because I don't want my quiet little life being interrupted with you and your questions and your drama, okay?"

He stands there in shock. I don't think I've ever said one word to Stevie let alone an entire paragraph. "Okay, then…" He trails off, still absolutely stunned by my admission. I turn to the door, and as I turn to open it, he slams it shut. "I'll keep asking Jolie." He reminds me. Which causes me to look at him. "You may think I'm a freak, but a girl like you, so quiet and innocent, you will surely have some skeletons in your closet you don't want people finding out."

I step back, away from him. "Are you threatening me?" I ask, but it comes out almost as a whisper.

"I'm warning you, Jolie. Let's make that clear." he says, pressing me against the back of the door in the janitor's closet. "I can see right through you. You may want to be invisible, but everyone sees you. You're hardly one to miss."

His eyes are filled with both annoyance, but also lust. His pupils are dark, hungry. He wants something and right now, I don't think it's a tutor.

"Stay away from me, Stevie. I mean it." I say before pushing him back and letting myself out of the closet. I head straight to my class, it's pretty much empty and I don't think I've ever been this late to my class for a while.

Thankfully, I head in through the back door to the class, and

I'm not the only one that's late. And not even a minute later, our teacher begins the lesson.

* * *

By lunch, I am using corridors I don't need to go down, just to avoid Stevie. I'm yet to see him since this morning, but his warning, as he said, is something that has been playing on my mind this morning. The only thing I have to hide is what I write. And unless he is willing to add breaking and entering to his rap sheet, I think I'm safe on that front.

I don't think I've ever been that close to a man that wasn't my dad or my brother. But also, I would hate to admit it, how turned on I got when he towered over me the way he did. I'm just a little over five foot four, and Stevie is at least six feet.

Even though I've been avoiding him because I don't want to deal with him, I'm also very uncertain of this feeling between my legs and how I keep having flashbacks to how he backed me against the door.

I think I just need to get laid, by anyone else but Stevie, or I just need to masturbate, either way that will calm my crazy thoughts.

Finally, after searching the sea of people in the cafeteria, I find my friend Lauren in a heated discussion with Donny, Stevie's friend.

"That's such bullshit!" I hear her exclaim as I approach the bench. "Elena would of chose Tom if Stefan hadn't come back to Mystic Falls."

Ah… one of Lauren's many passions. The Vampire Diaries. I have never really seen the show, but her room is filled with

Jolie

posters, memorabilia, and notebooks relating to the show.

"Stefan and Elena were endgame." Donny projects back, taking a stand. "Ah, and someone here might agree with me." He looks out on the sea of people. "Stevie!" He calls out and I feel my entire body go numb. Oh no.

"What's the topic?" He asks as he approaches the table, looking around, but then he notices me.

"The Vampire Diaries. Did Stefan and Elena deserve to be together." Donny says, but Stevie never breaks his eye contact with me.

"Nah man," he says as he pulls Donny closer. "I'm a Delena fan."

"Oh, come on!" Donny says, almost in disgust. Stevie ignores him, before coming and sitting next to me on the table.

"Have you given anymore thought into what I asked earlier?" He mutters under his breath.

I move away to avoid looking at him, getting my sandwich out of my bag and placing it on the table. "No."

I hear him sigh, but I don't dare to look up. "Did you feel the tension between us, Jolie?" He asks in my ear. I feel myself freezing up. "Cause, I did. And it was hot." The craving between my legs is only getting stronger, and I decide I'm best off moving a little away from him, but also ignoring him. "I reckon you're not as innocent as you look, you know." He says softly to just me. I begin to become conscious that someone can hear him as I look around, avoiding his eyes. "No one is listening to a thing I say." He almost reassures me, like this conversation is normal.

"Stevie, I'm not going to tutor you. I don't have time." I express harshly, but he frowns his brows.

"But Lauren said you were leaving your job, so you would

have time to tutor me." he explains, throwing Lauren under the bus. As I turn to give her a look of ' are you serious?' She's completely infatuated with Donny and what he is saying about some topic regarding a TV show. And then suddenly it makes sense. Lauren likes Donny. Fantastic.

"I'm not leaving my job, okay? I like my job. And I have too much family stuff going on right now to think about tutoring you."

Stevie sits back slightly. "Oh yes…" He says as he looks around. "Your brother's anniversary is coming up, isn't it?"

My heart completely stops, as does the world. Mainly because he almost announces it to the entire school that it will soon be the three years since my brother's death. "Get over yourself, Stevie." I say as I pick up my sandwich and my bag and make my way towards the front of the cafeteria.

I don't want him to come after me, or anyone else for that matter. Why can't I remain invisible, why does he and everyone else have to know my business?

Stevie

I've fucked up.

I knew I shouldn't have mentioned her brother, but it just slipped out. She dries her hands.

In all honesty I forgot completely until she said it.

Three years ago, Jolie's brother Isaac committed suicide. It had later came out that he was struggling with depression, and it sent him over the edge when he got accepted into the army.

The Masons were devastated, and so they should be. But with the death of a child in this town, comes a lot of vicious rumors about the family that weren't true.

Eventually, the rumors went away, mainly because not one of them said anything to disprove them, which didn't cause any traffic, and naturally, people moved on.

The only reason I'm after Jolie as my tutor is because of her friend Lauren. She's pretty worried about her at the job that she's in, but didn't really go into specifics.

Sal's Pizza Joint is the hottest spot in town if you're a teenager in high school or have a family. From what I've gathered, everyone goes there and because I hate people, I avoid a place like that.

I didn't see her again until school ended, and I watched her get into her petite little car and drive away as quickly as she could.

I head home too since I don't have band practice tonight and I try and think of a plan in order to get Jolie Mason to agree to tutor me.

It's not going to be easy, but there is something about her that just screams that she's hiding something. I've always noticed her, hell how could I not. She may not be Matilda George, who is the most average looking blonde haired white girl around, but she is Jolie Mason, and she is one hell of a looker. Her oversized jumpers and Mom jeans with her Nike Air Force 1's. She never stood out in a crowd to anyone else but me. And oddly enough she hates me, and I haven't really done anything to her… yet.

I still have two days to convince her to be my tutor, and although she's working tonight, I do want to give her the night off from me to think about it.

Anytime I got closer to her to smell the sweetness of strawberries and cream in her hair, it almost kept me intoxicated.

But the way she blushed anytime I got closer and the way she looked at me when I had her pinned against the door, wasn't a look of fear, she was giving me fuck me eyes.

And as I walk home thinking about it, it's getting me fucking horny and drunk off her. There are many reasons why she wouldn't find me attractive, I don't even know the girl. But fuck she would look good in my bed.

More than likely she will have something deep and dark that she's either into or that she's a virgin. Either way, both are hot.

Stevie

As I enter the front door, my dad is just on his way out. "Hey," he says as he quickly passes me. "Sorry I'm in a rush, it's bowling night and if I'm late your mother will kill me." He laughs as he heads to his car. "There is money on the table for a pizza and we will be out late. And please be good."

Without being able to say a word, he pulls out of the driveway and down the road towards the exit of our street.

Dad is an investment banker once musician, like me. And Mom works as Receptionist for a local law firm. Both high school sweethearts, had a kid young, but Mom always encouraged Dad to pursue his dreams, but because Dad had a lot of anxiety and sometimes used drugs as a form of self-medication. So, in the end decided that being in a band or a performer wasn't for him, and settled down for a quiet life with his family and became an investment banker instead. He was always good with numbers, or at least that's what he says. But as I grew up and found my own style, my dad was thrilled, but my mom wasn't too happy. She wanted me to fit in, but I had always been different growing up, and music was always something that I loved.

I decide to get a drink and head up to my room to play my guitar. While also thinking of ways to have Jolie Mason agree to tutor me. She will be stubborn, and tell me no, but her pretty little eyes were telling me something different.

And she may not like me, I don't care. But I am who I am because I always get what I want.

Jolie

I'm rushing around like a mad woman this morning.

My alarm never went off, so in order to not be publicly called out by Matilda, Brandon, and their crew, I need to leave in the next two minutes, and I barely look like a functioning human, more like an exhausted pigeon.

I grab the sheets of paper for my homework off my desk and put them in my bag before almost running out of the door. "Bye!" I shout to my parents who both stand up from the table to watch me run out of the door.

"Jolie, we need to talk about the trip!" I hear Dad call after me.

"Tonight, okay?" I say, stopping in my tracks to look at them. "I'm late for school."

My Mom shakes her head. "Jolie, this is for your brother, you can miss a few days of school to honor his memory."

"Mom, I'm late," I repeat. "Can we please talk about this later?"

She waves me away and I run out of the door to my car.

Jolie

Still trying to stick to the speed limit, I head towards the direction of the school, praying that there isn't any traffic.

I'm thankful that fifteen minutes later, I turn up at the car park at school. I grab my bag and head towards the entrance of the school.

"You're not one to be late." Lauren says as she greets me at the door.

"Don't get me started, my alarm never went off." I say, taking a drink out of my water bottle.

"You're fine, don't worry. They haven't even pulled into the car park." She explains, grabbing my arm.

"Thank god." I mutter. "And the more I avoid Stevie today, the better my life will be."

Lauren gives me a look and I manage to mirror it. "He likes you. That's why he's asking." She explains.

I begin to laugh like a mad woman. "Funny," I say, looking at her. "Sure, it's got nothing to do with the fact that you are drooling all over Donny?" I ask her, as we begin to walk through the hallway to our lockers.

She avoids my eyes. "No idea what you're talking about." She says in defense.

I still continue to laugh. "Sure, you don't. It's not like everyone around can sense the sexual tension between you, but I digress."

I open my locker and begin to empty everything into my locker. I don't need my homework till later, since History is this afternoon.

"Look, I'm single, lonely and in need of some good dick." Lauren explains, trying to make me understand her reasoning.

"And you thought Donny would give you that?" I almost laugh, to which she shoves me.

"Jolie, he has so many kinks it's insane."

I look to her with a smile. "Did you really think he would be vanilla?" I ask her and she rolls her eyes.

"Well, no, but I didn't think he would have so many kinks." She whispers as the hallway begins to get quiet. "I have bruises, Jolie. My ass, is sore."

I put my hand up to stop her from saying any more. "Lauren that's called assault, do I need to ring the police?" I ask her, with a smile and she shoves me lightly.

"One day you will no longer be the virgin Jolie and you'll come in with a smile on your face cause of some good dick."

I stop what I'm doing and look at her. "Well yeah, but I doubt that will be until I go to college, which I'm completely fine with." I say and she shrugs.

"Suit yourself, because from what I heard, Stevie is a freak is the streets and in the sheets." She winks and me, before walking away down the hall to her first class.

As I turn back to my locker, the familiar scent of tobacco and cologne is filling my nose and I take a long deep breath as I look to my feet to see Stevie's Doc Martins standing right next to mine.

"Fuck off, Stevie." I say harshly, gathering my things for my first class.

He peeks his head round to look at me with a pout on his face. "That's harsh."

I roll my eyes. "Trust me, it's nicer that what I really wanted to say. I'm not tutoring you, go away and bother someone else."

He moves to stand where Lauren just was to block me from my path. "Look, I know I was out of line yesterday. And I'm sorry," He apologizes. "But in order to do something in the summer that is going to change my life for the good, I need a

Jolie

tutor, and according to ninety percent of people in this school, you were the person that said would help me."

I look up to him, and the second I do, his eyes turn dark, and he stares down at me, like a predator hunting its prey. "No, Stevie." I repeat, but it almost comes out as a whisper.

"Are you sure?" He asks, his voice low and husky.

"Yes," I whisper. I have a determined look on my face, so he knows I'm serious and suddenly his eyes change from the deepest black to that soft hazel.

"I don't think, you're sure. But I do get what I want. So, you have till tomorrow to come up with a good enough reason as to why other than the fact I'm known as the *freak* and then we can go from there. Got it?" He asks me.

"Get over yourself, Stevie. You think that if you bat your eyes at me like I will fall like a domino and come to your defense. Well, I'm not going to do that. You have no respect for anyone but yourself, you're narcissistic, a ass hole and a obnoxious jerk. So, this is me telling you for the final time. I will not help you. Because, well... I don't want to."

I slam my locker shut and walk away.

I do hear him call after me, but I decide since I've stood my ground, and he should understand that no means no. I won't turn around to see what he wants.

Stevie

As she walks away, I notice a piece of paper that has fallen out of her locker. Not bothering to read it, I call after her, but she keeps walking, not bothering to turn around.

If I know something about Jolie Mason, it will be some sort of answers to homework that she's filled out that might help me in one of my classes.

As I begin to read it, I feel my mouth dry up and my dick twinge with excitement as my eyes glide over the filthy words on the page. Jolie Mason isn't no innocent after all.

The characters are going at it with each other in one of the raunchiest sex scenes I think I've ever read. She's riding him, and he's praising her, telling her how good she is to use him and how he wants to watch her cum all over his cock.

Fuck.

Jolie Mason writes complete filth. The dirtiest of stories regarding characters she's created. And by what I can see, the page continues because when I get to the bottom, the girl is just about the climax.

How the fuck am I meant to focus after reading that? The more I imagine it with one of my many one-night stands, the harder my cock gets.

I fold it up and put it in my jacket pocket for safe keeping. I'll give it to her later, and say I haven't read it when I have…

Or…I can use it to have her agree to tutor me. This is what she was hiding. The words of a completely horny, deranged woman. More than likely fantasies Jolie has thought of herself. Now that is hot.

I decide to go down the blackmail route, since I have nothing to lose. She clearly doesn't want anyone to find out about her little secret.

* * *

After science, I head in the direction of my friend Donny and Jolie's friend Lauren's direction. If I'm correct, they have a free period together which they use to have sex in one of the old buildings behind the school.

As I approach, I can hear what seems to be a belt meeting flesh and soft moans coming from who I'm assuming is Lauren. "Sorry guys, hate to intrude." I say as I approach. I don't look at them, only divert my eyes.

"What do you want Stevie?" Lauren asks harshly. I understand why I'm ruining her fun.

"I need Jolie's number please." I ask nicely and as I look up, my eyes or my brain was expecting what was right in front of me. Lauren dress in a rather raunchy Lady Macbeth dress and Donny dressed as Macbeth… with a wig.

I smile like a mad man at them. This might be better than finding out Jolie Mason does porn. Who knew they were into Shakespeare porn!

She gets up rather quickly and pulls her phone out, not bothering to look at me as she signals me to hand over mine. I do so, with the stupidest grin on my face. This is *fantastic*.

A couple of seconds later she shoos me away as does Donny handing me my phone, but before I go I turn back to them just as she reaches for his shirt. *"Unsex me here! And fill me from the crown to toe, top full of direst cruelty!"*

"Fuck you, Stevie!" Lauren shouts after me as I watch her reach for her shoe to throw me with it. Laughing, I make my way over to the old library where Esther, Donny and I hang out.

I pull out my phone again, and text Jolie in the hopes that she turns up.

'Meet me at the old library in 10 mins.'

As I go to put my phone in my pocket, it goes off again.

'Who is this?'

Cute. *'Someone who has something you might want.'*

As I enter the old library, I begin to get comfortable, waiting patiently for Jolie to arrive.

Deep down I do feel guilty for extorting her, but my… who knew that Jolie Mason was kinky. I sure didn't.

I look at my watch carefully as the minutes pass by ever so slowly. I gave her ten minutes, so surely, she should be nearly here.

And just as my mind asks the question, the door to the old library opens and I watch as a confused and slightly concerned Jolie enters.

"Hello?" She asks sheepishly as she walks through looking

along all of the rows of bookcases until I decide to make an appearance.

"Three minutes to spare, you're a good girl." I smile at her.

She cowers away from me. "Leading me into a space where we are alone? Classy. What do you want Stevie?" She asks harshly and I really don't like her tone.

"You know, you should be nice to me, considering in my pocket is something that could quite well ruin your life." I smugly say. "But if you do as I ask, I won't tell a soul."

She rolls her eyes. "Digging up fake dirt are you, Stevie?"

I laugh, like the joker. "Oh no, even I couldn't have made this up. My eyes were blessed this morning when I found it." I say reaching for my pocket and pulling out the piece of paper. "I grind my hips, feeling the weight of his cock touch my g-spot—" She launches herself at me to try and take it off my hands.

"Where the hell did you get that?" She asks, but it comes out as a whisper.

"If you had turned around when I called your name, Jolie, I wouldn't have found out your deepest darkest secret." I say coldly, crouching down to whisper in her ear. "Jolie Mason is a slutty book writer."

She looks to me out the corner of her eye. Her expression filled with rage and despair, and she battles to fight off the tears that are forming in her eyes. "So… you've turned to blackmailing now?" She asks me, almost disgusted by my behavior. "Did your time in prison not teach you anything?" She shouts at me.

"That wasn't my fault." I say in a way to defend myself. It wasn't in truth; it wasn't my fault at all.

"Not from what I heard." She snaps back.

"You weren't there. You don't have a say in what happened that night."

She steps back slightly almost as if she became afraid of me. "You're right. I don't know what happened. And I don't care."

"Good. I don't want you to care."

"Good."

She moves away from me, almost as if she's trying to think of what to do. "So, this is how you want to do this?" she asks harshly. "You're going to blackmail me to get what you want?"

I smile a little. "I wouldn't have had to go down this route if you had just said yes in the first place. But yes, and it's a hill I'm willing to die on."

She begins to pace down the walkway between bookcases. "Okay then Stevie, fine!" She explodes. "But if you're wanting this, I have some rules of my own."

I smile, realizing I really do have her where I want her. "Go on, I'm listening."

She walks towards me slowly, her eyes filled with rage. "You don't talk to me at all while we are in school. If you need something, it can wait."

"Deal-"

"I'm not done. Do not think for one second that you will be getting anything other than a tutor." I raise my eyebrows at the request. "That means no flirty looks, because the only thing that will do is make me want to punch you in your perfectly proportioned face."

I grin. "You think my face is perfect?" She rolls her eyes. "That's cute babe."

"Stop it."

"Stop what?"

She stares blankly at me. "That! The charm. It's awful. Stop

Stevie

it."

I sigh as I lean against one of the bookcases. "Fine. I will be on my best behavior."

"I'll believe that when I see it, but whatever." She says, picking up her bag that she dropped on the floor. "I have some family issues at the moment, so you'll have to deal with it. But I'll do this on the condition it's two days a week."

"Three."

"Why three?"

"Well, I'm failing in almost every subject, so I'm going to need all the help I can get." I admit honestly.

She sighs again, placing her hand over her mouth as she thinks about what to do. "Fine. Three days a week."

"And you quit your job at the pizzeria."

Her eyes widen. "How the hell is that your call?"

"Because I need you focused, and besides, my parents are going to pay you by the hour. Well more than what you were going to be earning a week at that fucking pizza place."

She sighs. "Well, I need to know how much."

"$20 a hour."

Her eyes widen. "Three hours a day, three days a week…"

"That's $180 a week, $720 a month if that helps. More than what Sal pays you."

Her eyebrows raise. "So, math isn't one of the subjects I need to tutor you on, got it."

"Oh no, I still need help. But I can do simple equations, I'm not an idiot." I say in my defense. She is quick to give me a look. "Don't bother answering that."

Jolie turns around and begins to walk out of the library. "See you tomorrow then!" I grin, and she turns just to roll her eyes at me.

"Whatever, Stevie."

"Pleasure doing business with you, kinky."

She tuns on her heels. "Don't call me that!"

"What?" It's true. You write kinky stories; your nickname is kinky."

"I'm allowed to call you freak then. Since you like to call me something I don't like."

I gasp in excitement. "Forget Beauty and the Beast, it's now kinky and the freak!"

She presses her lips together and closes her eyes. "No. Don't ever say that again."

"Why? Isn't that creative?" I laugh at her. This time, she heads for the door. This time not bothering to turn round. "See you tomorrow!"

Suddenly I'm left in silence, and although deep down I do feel guilty for what I've done to her, I have to put myself first. And if using Jolie is the way I can go on tour, then I'll be able to sleep peacefully at night.

Jolie

For the rest of the day, I feel nothing but rage and embarrassment.

I completely ignore Lauren knowing fair well the reason Stevie got my number is because she gave him it.

How the hell did I not notice that I had picked up a page this morning? And it had to be one of the worst and raunchiest scenes ever. Oh my god what a mess.

I ashamed that the person that found out was Stevie fucking Pritchard.

Which means deep down, my life is ruined even before it even started.

I'm quick to my car and out before I see anyone else. I need to take a bit of a breather while I really think on what I want to do. No matter how I want to look at this, I'm going to be tutoring Stevie until the final year exam. That's just confirmed.

One of my many worries is if he doesn't pass, blames me and still releases the chapter anyway.

Grr why did I put my name on it!

Shame is the only thing I feel as I decide to drive around town.

I can either hide forever from the embarrassment, or I can do as instructed and tutor Stevie.

$20 an hour may not seem like much to some people, but I'm barely earning $8 a hour at the pizzeria, and I do eight to ten hours at a time, on a weekend.

In theory this will be better for me, money-wise. But the only downside to it is I'm tutoring Stevie. And I would rather claw my own eyes out than have to look at that smug smile.

For the next hour, I drive around town trying to clear my head, but not the sick feeling in my stomach. The issue I have is that I don't feel as though I can trust Stevie, not even a little bit.

As I arrive home and pull into the driveway, my parents are waiting for me by the door. This is not what I need. I could really do without having this intervention.

"Where were you?" Mom screams at me. "We were about to send out a search party!"

I lightly roll my eyes heading through the front door. "That's a bit dramatic, don't you think, Mom?"

"We were worried sick, you're never out this late! Tell us where you were immediately!"

"I was tutoring someone!" I shout back, lying my ass off. "I've got a job as a tutor as I'm leaving the pizzeria."

She gasps in horror. "You love the pizzeria job, Jolie."

"I really don't. He pays unfairly, and this job means that I can earn more cash for myself. It's easy money." I head through to the kitchen, placing my bag down on the desk.

"Okay, and how many days will you be tutoring them?" she asks, crossing her arms. Dad stands there silently. Not

Jolie

bothering to say a word.

"Until they feel confident without me, but their grades are so bad, Mom. It's the least I can do."

She sighs, "Alright."

My eyes widen. "Is that it? No more fighting, you're fine with that?" I ask her honestly.

"Sure, I mean it sounds good. As long as you're happy with it."

Something begins to eat at me that this isn't the end of it. "One exception though." She says as I begin to walk away from the kitchen. There it is. I turn on my heels to look at her. "Whatever we want to do to honor Isaac, you will do with no questions and no talking back to me, do you understand? And you will not be going off to college."

My heart sinks. "Wait, so I can tutor someone to better their future, but can't go off to better my own?"

She frowns to me. "Exactly. I've lost one child. I'm not losing another."

I stand back away from her. The way she is acting, you would think that I'm a kid who gets in trouble constantly. All I'm asking is for a little bit of freedom, and she's keeping me on lock down.

"What happened to Isaac, was his choice. He didn't feel as though he had a way out. So, he took the worst one. I'm not my brother, so please don't keep me on a leash."

I head upstairs, ignoring both parents as they call out for me.

That was the end of it, I'm completely done pandering to their demands to cope with Isaac's death.

Isaac died because he committed suicide. Our parents since we were younger have been overbearing and controlling. To the point when Isaac didn't get accepted in the army and failed the test for the navy too, just down to poor planning, he decided it wasn't worth coming home to our parents to tell them the news.

Mom needed someone to blame of course, and instead of looking at herself in the mirror. She blamed me. Because I, in her mind, knew everything about my brother and could have prevented it.

The truth being Isaac and I weren't close. He was a little bit older, and during his time when we were both at the same school, tortured me in the hallway or anyway he could.

I still loved him though, even though he was bitter and nasty towards the end. I never wanted him to choose the way out that he did. I would have liked to think that I could have talked him out of it. But even thinking about that for hours while I grieved his death, I couldn't come up with a definitive answer to that budding question.

As I reach my room and lock my door, wanting to avoid my parents as much as possible. Placing my bag on the bed, I rush to my cupboard, desperately searching for that missing page in my manuscript. As I begin to put the pieces together, I notice that Stevie holds the missing page to my manuscript. FUCK!

I sit on my floor, completely stuck as to what to do. On the one hand, I can have my entire life ruined because of my parents and their need to control everything or have my life ruined by a curly-haired rocker. Either way, it's not going to end well for me.

* * *

The next day isn't as exciting, but instead agreeing to my

Jolie

parents' demands. I shouted as I left this morning that I'm leaving for school, and I am tutoring tonight. Hurrying to my car as I seen them run after me.

The positive to this is that Stevie seems to leave me alone, like I asked. Lauren had some questions, but when I asked her if she gave Stevie my number, she had managed to quickly shut up.

As I make my way to my car at the end of the day, I feel my phone buzz in my bag and as I reach for it, I notice a message from Stevie with his address. He doesn't live far from me, only about ten minutes in the car so that makes it easier.

I begin to make my way there, looking around at how much quieter this part of town is compared to my area. All the kids live in my area, or just outside, but this is a completely different kind of part to the town.

Mainly because the people who live here have some serious money. I really do wonder what Stevie's parents do in order to pay for a house like this.

Turning right, I get signaled that Stevie's house is on the right. And what a pretty house it is.

I know that Stevie doesn't have any siblings, but this house could sleep eight people, probably more. Curiosity begins to brew in me on how much money Stevie actually has.

As I pull into the driveway and get out of the car, I can't help but take in the beauty of the house. It looks like a cute white farmhouse. But when you drive round, you can see it goes on forever.

I watch the door open, and not even a second later, Stevie appears with a smile on his face. He was waiting for me… fantastic.

"Took you long enough." He teases, which I ignore as I reach him. "Come on, kinky."

I follow him into the house, and as I enter, it is the most beautifully aesthetic home that I've seen in person, other than Pinterest.

"Where is your lair?" I ask him, a firm look on my face to show him I'm not kidding.

He smiles. "Upstairs," he says, heading towards them. "Come on." He ushers. I follow him up the stairs, unsure on what is about to greet me.

To the left of the staircase, is a long hallway, and at the end of that is clearly Stevie's room. Posters, a FUCK OFF sign and a large sticker of his band Death Due practically covers the door. "I see this is your den." I smirk, to which he joins in. "Do you sleep in a coffin like the rumors?"

As he stops at the door, he grins to me. "I have a big enough coffin for the two of us, Jolie; care to join me in the world of the undead?"

I almost want to cringe, but for some reason, my cheeks begin to flush as I find any reason to avoid his eyes. "God no."

He mutters something under his breath which I ignore, and opens the door to reveal his bedroom, which isn't a surprise. Guitars, a drum kit, a microphone, and a sound booth are in one corner of the room. The room to the left looks to be a bathroom from what I can see. But Stevie's room is dark, just as I suspect his heart is.

"Don't be shy." He says as he takes a seat at his desk. "Come on in."

There isn't a coffin, or the heads and body parts of small children as I expected. It is just Stevie's creativity within these walls.

Posters from the likes of Bon Jovi, Metallica and The Police are plastered on his walls and as I begin to look closer to the pieces of paper that he seems to have stuck on with tape, it looks to be song lyrics.

"I have a lot of creative spells if you will. When music takes over and it's the only thing that I can focus on." He explains, looking right at me. "Are you disappointed?" He frowns, and I turn back to look at the words on the wall.

"A little." I admit honestly. "But then if it was as plain and boring as most other guy's rooms, I would have been alarmed."

He grins. "Have you been in a lot of boys rooms, kinky?"

I roll my eyes. "No. But even if I had I wouldn't tell you."

He pulls up a chair and taps it, telling me to sit down. "I don't bite."

I can't stop the laugh from leaving my throat. "That's a lie. I've heard you've got quite the biting fetish."

I look at him, and his eyes are a playful shade. He's not denying it either, although it was a rumor going around the school for a while. A girl who left our school, Tabitha, I think her name was, slept with Stevie a year ago. She said he had some interesting kinks, something no one actually disagreed with her on. He's known as the freak, so why wouldn't he have a long list of unusual kinks?

"Moving on," I say as my cheeks begin to turn red. "What classes are you struggling with?"

He sits back in his chair thinking for a second. "All of them." He says honestly.

My eyes widen. "I thought you were kidding?" I ask him and he shakes his head.

"No, kinky. I'm not. I don't know how I've made it this far in high school, but I would like to be able to tour with my band over the summer. And you're gonna make that happen."

I raise my eyebrow at him. "But if you've never had a reason to work hard, why now? What happens if you're completely incapable of learning anything?"

He leans closer to me so I can now smell his cologne. "Then you're a shit tutor then, aren't you?"

"Funny." I narrow my eyes as I begin to get the items I'll need out of my bag. "You'll need to clean your desk. I will need somewhere to teach you, and a table full of song lyrics and musical notes isn't my ideal tutoring space."

Reluctantly, he begins to pick up the lyrics and pieces of paper in bulk as he carries them over to his bed or to another space.

Without another word, he sits down, frowning almost as I begin to get myself prepared. "Why is everything in order? That annoys me." He huffs and I turn my head to glare at him.

"If you have everything in order, your life will go the same way. Let's take your life for example Stevie. It's a dumpster fire. You live in chaos because you are chaotic, you don't have an off switch and you don't know when to listen. Whereas I, listen, take notes, and have my life in order. You don't want to learn because you don't think you'll need it. Whereas I want to go to college and get a job in the real world. But all you'll be doing is chasing the high of being a small band in a small town and not really go anywhere."

For the first time ever, Stevie is silent. Not sure what to say. And the quiet makes me feel both nervous and proud of myself. Stevie expects so much from so many people, so it's no surprise that he has resorted to blackmail in order to get something that he wants. "Let me see your class schedule." I ask and he unpins it from the board in front of us and hands me it. "Okay, so you're taking biology, history and music as well as an extra in

Jolie

creative writing?" I ask almost stunned. "If you're in creative writing, why aren't you in my class?"

He avoids my eyes for a second as he clears his throat. "I got moved out of that class before it even started. I have another teacher. Mr. Phillips... well I slept with his daughter, and he walked in on it. Let's just say we avoid each other."

I press my lips together so hard that I can feel them turn white. I'm trying not to laugh at this, and it seems to have somewhat traumatized Stevie. So, I try my hardest to get my laughter under control. Clearing my throat, I pull out my notebook and the textbook we will need.

"Okay, let's start with history, although I'm in a higher class, the syllabus is pretty much the same. We will spend a hour going through it and then take a little break and move onto something else, okay?"

He nods. Not saying another word as he moves closer. His face is only inches away from mine as he looks directly at the book, not even acknowledging my stare. I decide to focus on the topic and begin to explain the topic to him. He listens carefully, only asking questions if I explain something too quick, but mainly just takes notes.

* * *

After history, we moved onto a biology, and I very quickly realized this is the topic Stevie is going to struggle with the most.

We decide to take a break as he grabs us a can of soda from the fridge, and he begins to ask me questions as we go over what he has learned today.

"This arrangement feels good." He explains taking a sip of his cherry cola. "The way you explain things is so much better than the teachers. You wait until I understand it, rather than move over to the next topic."

I smile. "It's easier that way, which means you'll want to understand it."

"Yeah, good manipulation tactic."

I laugh. "I'll start using some of your tactics. Then I'll become a freak to society."

"Best way to be."

I avoid his eyes, not realizing the words that have just left my mouth. "Sorry, that was mean—"

"It's okay. I'm used to it. In fact, I don't mind it. It used to bother me. Not so much anymore." I smile, feeling a little bit at ease knowing that he isn't going to hold it against me. I still don't like him, but I feel like this arrangement can be good for both of us even if it only came about because he blackmailed me. "Just means I can call you kinky."

I roll my eyes. "Please don't…"

"Why? Is it because you know it's true?"

I begin to blush. "I'm not as kinky as you think I am."

"Oh?" He says playfully. "You sure about that? Or is it what you read too?"

Just as I'm about to answer, I hear the door behind me open and a conversation between a man and a woman, who I'm assuming is Stevie's parents, continues. As they walk towards us, just finishing off their conversation, they greet me with a smile. "Hello." They say as the woman places her bags down and extends her hand. "I'm Candice and this is my husband, John." She introduces them both as I go to shake his hand also.

"Nice to meet you. I'm Jolie, Stevie's new tutor."

Jolie

Her eyes widen with surprise as she looks to Stevie who stands behind the kitchen counter. "Well, you were not what I was expecting." She admits honestly. "But I am very pleased to meet you." She grins to me.

"What my wife means to say is that the nerds and the brighter kids in school were more..."

"Geeky looking?"

They exchanged a look between each other. "No..." They say in defense, but you can tell that it was exactly what they meant.

"It's okay. Geeks look a little bit like me." I smile a little.

It seems to reassure the mood somewhat as they take a seat beside me, and Stevie grabs them both a drink.

"Jolie, we really appreciate you tutoring Stevie so he can pass his exam at the end of the year."

I smile. "It's no problem." I turn to look at Stevie. "After he explained why he needed a tutor and why he wanted me to help him, I couldn't really say no. It's a really big opportunity."

Stevie glares at me, knowing exactly what I'm meaning by that.

"Exactly, and as much as I would wish he would get a normal job like John did in the end, I always knew deep down that Stevie would follow in his footsteps. Music is one of his many talents."

I smile at them. "So, I've heard."

"So," Candace says, wanting to change the subject. "Are you guy's friends?"

"No." Stevie and I answer in sync almost immediately. "Lauren, Jolie's friend, is dating Donny, Mom." Stevie explains and internally I thank him for his quick response.

"We didn't really know each other. Only briefly passing in the school hallways."

"Well, I'm pleased he found you. You seem as though you will become friends."

Stevie just smiles at me, but the look on my face tells him everything he needs to know. I have no intention of ever being his friend.

After a small conversation getting to know his parents, I head for the door as they say goodbye. "So, see you tomorrow?" Stevie asks softly as he walks me to the door.

"Yep. See you tomorrow."

I open the door, making sure not to look back as I head towards my car. But suddenly, as I open the car door, I find my eyes locked with Stevie's as he waves goodbye. Suddenly I feel butterflies rush to my stomach and a wave of nausea right after it.

Rushing into my car and pulling out of the driveway, I head home trying to get my thoughts in order.

Stevie

It's been almost a month since Jolie has been tutoring me. And I think it's going super well. The agreement with my parents is that she gets paid weekly in cash, and today, I get a report from Mr. Franks to see if my grades are improving.

Even if they are, I don't want Jolie to leave just yet as I'm worried, I'll fall back into my old ways. The way she explains things so much clearer than any teacher, it makes me look forward to her tutoring me.

I've tried to have conversations with her about the chapter that I found, but she dodges the question or her slightly tanned skin turns a bright shade of red.

She's either a virgin or she's vanilla during sex. But I've found that the quieter girls who read books are always the ones with more flavor. I would love to know what her body count is, or what she's even done with a man before. I think the uncertainty is eating at me.

Sometimes when she leaves my room after we have been studying, it smells like her. And it makes me sad, but also excited for the next day I see her.

I find her ridiculously attractive. But the last thing I want to do is start up a sexual relationship and then it all goes to shit because I fuck it up. Which I'm known to do.

I head in the direction of Mr. Franks classroom, making sure to take the long way just so I can see Jolie for even a split second.

I'm not a simp by any means, but do I like to pass her in the hallway just to see her and her smile? Maybe.

As I turn left at the corridor, I notice her stand next to Lauren, deep in conversation about God knows what. I briefly look at her as I pass, this time she locks eyes for only a second and I feel my heart suddenly come to stop.

I look away first, not wanting to walk into anybody, or anyone I don't want to be associated with right now. I have butterflies in my stomach and a small smile on my face that I hope nobody can see.

Eventually, I make it to Mr. Franks classroom and as he finishes off his lunch, he notices me at the door. "Stevie!" He exclaims with excitement, mouth full of apple. "Come in, have a seat."

"Did you manage to get my results back?" I ask, placing my backpack on the floor.

"Yes, actually and I have to say I'm impressed."

My eyes widen. "Really?"

"Yes. Your grades are improving, Stevie." He hands me a piece of paper that does indeed conclude that my grades are improving. "Who did you manage to put under a spell to tutor you?" He asks, finishing off his apple.

"Jolie Mason." I say, not taking my eyes off the sheet of paper.

"Wow…" He says slowly, which does cause me to look up.

"Jolie is a nice girl. I'm pleased you got her to tutor you." He says, trying to ease some of the tension that has suddenly built up in the room.

"You know her?" I ask, placing the piece of paper down on the desk.

"I do." He admits taking a seat at the front of his desk. "I am friends with her father."

My eyes widen. "Wow." I say in shock.

"Yeah. We have been friends for over twenty-five years. My daughter, goes to a different school, but Jolie and Samantha were born on the same week on the same year."

I nod my head, unsure on what to do with the information.

"So, if Jolie keeps tutoring me, do you think I'll pass the exam?" I ask him honestly.

He smiles softly at me. "I do."

That's all he ever needed to say, which makes me feel thankful as I sit at this desk looking at the piece of paper. It's not a massive improvement, but I've almost gone up an entire grade in three subjects in a month.

I normally don't want to listen, hell, I barely want to learn, but she makes me want to learn. With the tour aside, it's exciting knowing that she's the reason I'm doing better in school.

Thanks, Mr. Franks." I say as I head towards his door, still staring at the piece of paper in my hand. There' only a few more hours left of school, and as much as I want to tell her the good news, I decide to hold off until I see her later.

* * *

I practically run home in anticipation to see both my parents and to see Jolie. She normally heads straight here after school, but she said she had to stop at home before heading to my place.

As I enter the front door, I'm greeted with my parents, who are currently on their way out. "Hey, son." Dad greets me. He's dressed in a suit, his hair slicked back and he's wearing his Rolex. Mom is dressed in a red dress, red lipstick that brings out the color of her eyes.

"Where are you off to?" I ask as they practically push past me.

"It's the annual ball, didn't we tell you?" Mom says with a smile.

No. "Yes. Sorry, I forgot."

They exchange confused looks between each other. "You seem like you're excited about something?"

I mean that's an understatement. "Don't worry, it can wait." I say with a reassuring smile. "Enjoy."

She gives me a kiss on the cheek before they head out of the door and towards the car. Mom is a receptionist, but every year they both get invited to the company's annual ball to talk about some boring adult shit that I won't even understand, and I don't want to.

Just as they begin to pull out of the driveway, Jolie parks up and gives my parents a wave. Getting her books out of the car, she gives me a concerning look, "Why do your parents look like James Bond and a bond girl?" She giggles with a smile.

I lean down to take some of the books off her as they look heavy. "Annual ball for Mom's work." I explain, inviting her in and shutting the door. "I don't tend to ask that many questions."

Placing the books down on the side and ignoring the look from Jolie, I pull the piece of paper out of my pocket. "What's

Stevie

this?" I hear her ask softly. Without saying a word, I hand it to her, and I watch as her face reads over the grades and the words and her eyes widen and a big smile grows on her face. "Stevie! This is great!"

"Yeah, I thought I would tell you."

She smiles softly at me, and as I look around her face, I notice a small dimple on her cheek. "Well, this is great news." She says handing me back the piece of paper. "Means I can get back to normal sooner." Jolie grins, picking up the books behind me, and heads towards the stairs.

"You love this arrangement, don't lie." I say passing her on the stairs and walking backwards as I look down to her.

"You wish, now come on. I don't have all day."

For the next two hours we discuss a bunch of different topics that might come across in the final test, as well as some personal things. She still seems very closed off, but slowly and surely, I can see her begin to open up to me.

It's nice.

I know that deep down I'm probably only looking for a one-night stand, but something about her tells me that she's different, and not because she writes kinky stories.

"So..." I say as I answer the last question on her little test. "Care to tell me the story of Daniel and India?"

She doesn't look at me as she takes the paper out of my hands and begins to look over my answers. She remains quiet for a few more seconds before she speaks, "I really don't want to talk about it, Stevie."

Although I can feel the tension brewing in the air, I decide to press her for more. "You know, a lot of what you said isn't right."

Her eyes dart up to look at mine. "What do you mean?" She

snaps.

"Well, the positions you have the characters in, it doesn't give the most pleasure. Just saying."

Jolie sits back for a moment, staring at me wide eyed. "And you would know this, how?"

I grin. "Trust me, I'd know."

She rolls her eyes. "So, what? I'm meant to use you for inspiration now, get all of my facts from you?"

I shrug my shoulders, "It would make sense that you fact check to too." I say leaning closer towards her. "Say you did extensive research…"

She pushes me away and begins to pack her bags. "Screw you, Stevie." And not a second later she is out of the door and down the stairs.

Sitting stunned at my desk for a moment trying to process the situation that has just occurred. I do feel a strong sense of guilt flow over me.

But her outburst confirmed one thing tonight. Jolie Mason is a virgin.

Jolie

I've barely slept.

And not because I'm mad at Stevie for embarrassing me. I'm mad because when I went over the chapter and how it went in my head, and how I think I wrote it.

He was fucking right!

It didn't make sense, and it didn't give them any pleasure at all.

Now, I'll never admit out loud how Stevie was right, but all it means is that when I ask him about it tonight, he has to tell me.

School was nothing new, and because I barely got noticed, I obviously didn't get picked on. The perks of being quiet, but good in school.

I didn't even see Stevie today. Although he would admit it, I noticed him come to check and see if I'm in school outside my locker when he heads to one of his classes.

As I pull up to Stevie's drive, I do see him hide behind his bedroom curtain, hiding, like a child waiting for the parents to come home. As usual, his parents aren't home. They are always out, but that must be the luxury of being wealthy, and the fact that their son gets in more trouble than anyone in town, I doubt they care anymore.

"I didn't think you'd come." I hear him say as he opens the door to greet me. "I'm sorry about yesterday,"

I look up at him, stunned by his apology. "Well, I didn't think you had it in you."

He frowns at his bushy brows that hide behind his hair. "What?"

"Empathy and compassion. It's weird."

I move past him and make my way up the stairs, hearing him trail behind me like a lost dog.

"So, you're not mad?" He asks as we enter the room and I come to a stop.

"Not anymore."

"So, you were mad?"

"Yes."

"Pleased we've established that." he says with a sarcastic glance.

I sigh, placing the books on the desk. "I'm mad that you made me realize that I was wrong."

"I don't like it when you tell me I'm right."

"Me either." I am quick to respond. "I can feel the rash begin to burn into my skin."

"You know you should see a specialist for that."

I growl. "Stevie, tell me what I did wrong and how to make it right!"

He stands, stunned. I can see his eyes wander my face wondering if I'm asking him that exact question. "You want me to tell you? Or show you?"

Jolie

I pause, yet I can feel my face burn hotter than a thousand suns. "I-er. Not show. Just tell me." I say taking a seat at his desk, avoiding his direct eye contact. I ask the questions. You provide the answers."

"Okay," I hear him say from across the room, his voice low as if he's afraid to say anything else.

He sits beside me on the other chair, I can hear the chains from his pants hit it ever so slightly to make the slightest noise. His long-sleeved band t-shirt hangs over his arms as it's just that little bit too long for him.

"What would you recommend I change it to?"

"Well, missionary is simple yet effective." He says casually like this is just some normal conversation regarding the French Revolution.

I head over to my bag and pick up the bits I have folded up to hide from the rest of the world.

I bring them over to him sheepishly, like he's going to judge. But he doesn't. He simply takes them out of my hand and pulls the chair closer to me indicating I sit down while he reads.

For the next ten minutes, we sit in silence while Stevie reads the entire chapter, at least twice.

"Well," he says a moment or too later. "Points for being-" he begins to say but suddenly stops.

"What?" I ask eagerly, leaning in.

"Descriptive." He says, clearing his throat.

"Oh." I say after a second. "So that's not bad?" I ask to which he shakes his head.

"No, it's good, really good. But there are a few things I would change to maybe make it just that little bit better for your readers." He explains honestly.

I lean in closer. "Well, what is it?"

He closes his eyes and takes a long deep breath. "Jolie, please move back just a little you're distracting me." He growls lightly.

I'm taken by surprise but do exactly as he instructs as I stare at him, uncertain as what is going on. "I didn't mean to snap, it's nothing. Sorry, continue." He encourages me like he didn't just speak to me like that.

"Somethings wrong, so how about you tell me what is going on?" I ask, sass in my throat.

"Drop it, Jolie." He demands. "Do you want me to help you?" He asks again.

Instead of fighting with him, I nod, deciding it's not worth it.

"So, what do you reckon I do? Change some of the positions?"

He nods his head. "Yeah. I think that would be good, but also add in a bit of you know…" he says while looking up at me. His eyes are telling me I should know this answer, but my mind turns blank. "Kinkier."

I roll my eyes. "This is as kinky as I go."

"Dirty talk and a bit of choking, kinky, is barely anything. You need him to have something about him that makes him different, otherwise he's just another lowlife who's into meaningless sex with woman and doesn't care about the pleasure of his partner."

I turn my head in confusion. "I don't understand…"

"Okay," he says while pulling my chair closer to him to we are staring right at each other, only inches apart. "You want Daniel to be the reason India loves sex. That's how you've described it beforehand, but the actual sex scene shows him as selfish and pathetic. I mean I'm the reader, and all it shows is that he cares about his own pleasure than he does about India's which makes him a jerk."

"But he passionately kisses her…" I object and he holds his

hand up to stop me from continuing.

"Just because he's kissing her like that doesn't mean he cares about her in the way he should. He should want to watch her fall apart underneath him, become breathless so that she is grasping for that last little bit of air that she has left inside of her. Listen to her scream his name over and over again as she cums for the eighth time."

My mouth is wide open in shock while he seductively explains it. "You want her to come completely undone for him?"

"It's the only way your readers are gonna know he is a god in bed. Because right now, in the way I'm reading it, he lasts two minutes, India doesn't get a ounce of pleasure and she will be using her vibrator later."

I blink repeatedly. "He's good in bed." I protest trying to defend my character.

"Jolie, I put Daniel to shame, so for the love of fucking god, listen to me."

I go to protest again, but I find that no words come out, Stevie the freak has rendered me speechless. A new record.

"I'm not just talking about his lack of compassion for his sexual partner and her pleasure. I'm saying that watching someone feel the way they do knowing you did it to them. Creates a whole new kink in itself."

"And what kinks do you have that I don't know about?" I ask without thinking.

Although the second the words left my mouth, I felt guilty, deep down I really wanted to know what Stevie is into.

"Do you really want to know?" He asks, leaning down to me, placing his hands on my thighs as he looks deep into my eyes. I nod, not wanting to say a word but he sighs, dropping his head slightly to look at the floor. "One of my many kinks Jolie is I need consent, and you nodding your head; doesn't count. So, I'm going to ask you again. Do you really want to know?"

I nod my head, but only because I find myself struggling to speak as my mouth has gone so dry. "Yes." I managed to say eventually.

He lets go of his grip around my legs and sits back. "My list is very different unless you're into dark romance and have a long list of kinks yourself." He begins to explain. I sit, listening, waiting eagerly as he gets comfortable to continue - "For starters, do you think the masks in my room are for decoration?" He asks, not a smile on his face for once, which means he is serious.

I have a slight look around his room, and on one side of his wall, he has a Ghost face mask, Michael Myers and another one I don't seem to recognize.

"What's that one?"

"Have you never seen Ghost from Call of Duty?" I shake my head. He stands from the chair and makes his way over to the wall to pick it up. "I don't like a lot of video games, but I heard on a forum that Ghost, he opens the door to something darker." He explains, handing me the mask to look at. "With the likes of Ghost face and Myers, they're real people. But Ghost is different, he's an animation that woman seem to have some sort of sexual attraction to. It works a treat if you can get your voice right." He winks.

I look back down at the mask, not wondering whether it would be unusual to have a mask kink, but more would I find that attractive.

I had never read anything like what Stevie is describing. I'm sure they exist, but mask kinks. People get off with the person

Jolie

they are sleeping with pretending to be someone else?

"Next, "he says to get my attention, "I have the usual; I like choking. I like watching you think you're about to take your last breath while I'm fucking you uncontrollably, but in the right position so that I hit that sweet spot every single time."

"You won't be able to hit it every time." I say smugly. "Not every man can find it."

"Is that how it was for you, Jolie?" he asks, placing his hand back on my thighs as he leans in closer, a very small smile on his face. "Did he cum into the couch thinking it was your sweet little clit?"

My cheeks begin to heat up again, and because I'm in a state of shock. "I-I've never."

"I knew it." He says with a stupid smile. "But don't worry, by the time we've finished our little arrangement, you'll be well educated, as will I." He lets go on my legs, yet I can still feel his touch burn my skin.

"Lastly, I'm into BDSM." He says so casually while also changing the subject from the fact he just found out I was a virgin, back to his list of kinks. "Do you know what it means, Jolie?" He asks, to which I nod my head.

"Bondage, domination, submission and masochism." He grins at me.

"Good girl." He says while making his way over to his bed. "Oh, and also I like giving praise, but also giving pleasure." He says, as he leans back. "Let's just say I'm a giver rather than a receiver."

"So, that's what you're into?" I ask honestly and he nods at me.

"You seem disappointed, Jolie? Did you want me to tell you I'm into orgies and I have a sex dungeon somewhere in the house?" he raises one eyebrow.

"You don't have a sex dungeon."

"Wrong." He says quickly. "My parents never come in my room, so a lot of what I use on my sexual partners is hidden by different things."

"I see." I say quietly while looking around his room. "You can tell me if this is too much, but how many sexual partners have you had?" I ask curiously as I feel between my legs cry with need. I'm horny, and all of this talk with Stevie is making me what to do bad things. Either to myself later, or with him. Either way, with how I'm feeling I don't even believe I would regret it. My mouth is so dry, and because I've never felt this way before other than when I'm writing or fantasizing, it's hard for me to process this need. This want, to feel completely helpless while having someone dominate me.

"Six." he says which seems to break me out of my thoughts. "I've had six."

I nod, not wanting to say another word as I now feel embarrassed for asking him that question.

I can suddenly feel him move in front of me and I watch as he kneels to me, pressing his hands back of my thighs I feel as though I'm going to explode. "What do you want, Jolie?" He asks me, his voice low as I feel the rings on his fingers dig deep to my skin. "Tell me, what do you want?" he repeats. "Tell me," He pleads.

If I wasn't sat down, I would feel my knees buckle below me. He's begging. And since I am so horny like a cat in heat, I want him to keep begging, begging me to continue, begging me to stop, begging me to cum.

I'm craving it, to hear Stevie Pritchard cry out for me. "I-." I say trying to gather my thoughts as I begin to see images in

Jolie

my head of what could be if I let it happen. "I-"

"Use your words, Jolie." He says, lifting my chin to look at him. FUCK.

"I- I can't find the words." I say eventually feeling my body become hotter and hotter as the images become more and more intense.

"You know what you want, but I need you to tell me." He please again. He leans in closer, so close that our lips are practically touching at this point. "Tell me baby, please."

I close my eyes, hoping he will just kiss me, praying that it releases some of the tension going on between my legs. But he remains there, waiting for me to fucking speak, "Stevie, please."

"Not until you tell me what you want." he says against my lips. "Because you want something to give you that release."

It's like he is reading my mind and my eyes flutter open as I move away. "What?" I ask.

"Jolie, you have a craving that is so much stronger than anyone else. You want to find that release because no matter what you do, it's never going to be enough. Until one day it happens."

"So, what are you saying? You're not going to be that person?" I ask, my tone more annoyed this time as I feel my need simmer within.

"Oh, I'll be that person, fuck yes. But you need to want it just as much as me, and it's a big thing, so make sure you're actually ready." He speaks.

Although he is giving me a harsh truth, I can't help but feel kind of grateful that Stevie cared so much about my consent.

I've heard that most guys will just take advantage no matter if you eventually decide to change your mind and although I can feel myself become angry because I'm not chasing my release, I also know Stevie's right and I'm not ready.

"One day you'll be able to say that this is based on true events, kinky. That day might be soon. And wouldn't you rather lose your virginity to someone who actually cares, rather than some dick he couldn't care about you or your pleasure?" He asks me as he sits back on his chair.

"You're right."

"Hell, I might not end up being the guy you choose in the end. But just remember, just because he's interested in you, doesn't mean he actually cares about you."

I frown. "And you care about me?" I ask as I open up the textbook.

"Oh no, I couldn't give a damn." He says harshly, but I can see the smile slowly grow on his face.

"Yeah okay, freak. Next topic, get your notebook."

Stevie

I'm getting somewhere with her.

For the last week, we've had another great arrangement. She asks me all of the questions she wants, and I get to explain them to her, while she also teaches me the subjects I need to know about. I know she's not ready, I just wish she would say that. And after last week, how close I came to kissing her without her consent, I've had to be more restrictive with what I say and do with her.

I know she's desperate to chase her release. As a woman, but also as a virgin, it's kind of a need in a way. But her body language, her expressions, and the fact I could feel her wanting to press her legs together. That was getting me excited, knowing how turned on she was.

She avoided me during school, but when we're together she asks question after question while also letting me touch her legs or show her certain things without getting her too aroused.

I have another test this week to see how I'm getting on with my tutoring, and I also mentioned to my parents about the spike in my grades and they were thrilled. They brought Jolie and I pizza one night to celebrate. She only likes tomato and cheese, and no other toppings. Just plain. How ironic.

The more I avoid the pain in my asses the more my life seems to be getting just that little bit easier.

A new kid joined the school, and he has been the sole focus on their bullying for quite a few weeks, which has meant I have enjoyed some peace and quiet.

That's a lie. I fucking hate it.

It makes me feel as though I'm losing my charm as the local freak. Yet I have been slightly distracted by the smutty bookworm who catches my eye every time I walk the hall.

Who knew that a woman like Jolie Mason would make me feel in such a way. It's ironic, but also terrifying.

Band practice is tonight, and much to my parent's disagreement, they had to sign the forms to let me go on tour with Defending You Forever, on the agreement I still pass this end of year exam. Which I have every intention to. Because then none of this would be worth it.

"Stevie!" I hear a voice call after me. No one wants to talk to me in the school hall, so who the hell could be wanting my attention. As I turn to see who it is, I'm greeted with a blow to the face, and I feel myself fall and hit the floor.

My ears are ringing, and as I lift my hand up to see the damage, which is when I notice the blood. Ever so slightly, I can hear the annoying giggles of Matilda and her little group of friends as Brandon stands over me, spitting on me like I am the most disgusting thing in the world.

Teachers, the principal, and my fellow peers stand around watching as I get kicked once again, this time to my stomach causing me to fall back to the floor, blood coming out of both of my nose and mouth.

"Freak!" They shout, before I hear the school bell, and everyone begins to head towards their classes, completely standing over me to avoid being late. The teachers go back into their classroom, and the principal goes back into his office. They couldn't care. They've *never* cared about their students.

As the hallway begins to clear, I feel the pain from the initial punch come and hit me like a truck. "Fuck." I wince as I manage to rise to my knees. And as I look down the long and narrow hallway, that's when I see her, walking quickly towards me.

"Stevie?" She asks as she approaches me. "Are you okay? Oh my god." Jolie says as she lifts me up, placing my arm around her shoulder.

"Shouldn't you be in class?" I cough, blood coming out of everywhere. Really attractive, Stevie well done.

"I have a free period, I normally just study, but Lauren text me and I ran over from the library." She explains as we head behind us towards the male toilets. "In here, let's clean you up." She says, opening the door for me, while instructing me to sit on the sink while she gets some paper towels and the first aid kit from the corner.

"You know you're breaking the agreement." I smile at her, but the only thing I can taste is the copper from the blood.

"Shut up, or I'll let you bleed out, Stevie." She snaps at me as she begins to clean me up.

"Look at you, you care about me."

"Hmm, don't get used to it." She smiles while I feel her apply pressure to whatever wound is on my eye. I wince at the pain and out of my other eye, I watch as she carefully releases the pressure ever so slightly.

"Sorry, but this is going to stop the bleeding." She says as she applies the same amount of pressure yet again.

"Is it not because you like hurting me?" I ask her honestly and she gives me a look.

"Trust me, if I wanted to hurt you, I'd try a little harder." she teases. "However, I think you've had enough for today, so I'll be nicer."

As I look down to her, I notice today how her hair is different and how she's added more sparkle to her eye shadow than normal.

"Thank you." I say softly, while looking deep into her eyes. "I mean it, I would have had to find someone to clean me up who wouldn't mind being a target for two days, but you came out of your study session to help me. That means more than you know."

She gives me a weak smile. "I hope they haven't knocked some sense into you." she says sarcastically. "It's disappointing if they have, I liked it when you were clueless and only had empathy when you wanted something."

I laugh. "I'm still me, but with a black eye and I think…" I say as I move my tongue around my mouth checking for gaps. "All of my teeth."

She laughs this time, shaking her head, avoiding my eyes. "You know, Stevie; you're not as scary as people think you are."

I grin, raising my hand slightly, to move the hair that has fallen in front of her face. "And you, Jolie Mason, are not as invisible as you think you are."

We stare into each other's eyes for what seems like forever, and for how long it is, I'm grateful no one comes in to ruin the moment.

She looks away first and for some reason, I feel my heart hurt as she begins to get rid of the bloody tissues and wipes the countertop in the men's bathroom.

"I need to have a look at your stomach and see how much damage they've done." She says as she gets closer to me again and I can become engulfed in the sweet smell of her fruity perfume.

"If you want to see me shirtless kinky, all you had to do is ask." I tease.

Instead of joining in this time, she rolls her eyes and I lift up my shirt to reveal a large red mark that will one day soon, become a bruise. "That's gonna leave a beautiful mark." She says as she begins to inspect it. "But it seems to me that you're alright otherwise." She moves her hair out of the way as she pulls my shirt down for me. "You purposely flexed by the way." she teases as she goes to wash her hands,

"Actually," I say which gets her attention to look right at me. "I'm not."

Her eyebrows raise as she continues to wash her hands. Jail taught me one thing, and that is to stand up for myself. The only issue that I have with that is I can't hit my bully's because it will put me back into jail.

"What are you doing for the rest of your free period?" I ask her softly as she dries hands with a paper towel.

"Well, I have some things to do for my college applications, so I will probably do that." She says, walking over to collect her bag. "You're going back to class." She instructs, and I feel myself frown.

"Huh?" I ask her, confused. "I can't go to class; I've missed the first ten minutes." I explain, as if she's, my parent.

"Yeah, well Stevie, life is a bitch and then you die. If you want to pass this test at the end of the year, you have to go to your classes. I'm sure the teacher will be fine with it."

Instead of pouting, I decide to do as I'm told and follow her out of the bathroom.

The hallway is still quiet, not a person in sight.

"I'll see you tomorrow?" I ask her as she begins to walk back in the direction of the library.

"See you tomorrow."

Jolie

After yesterday's events, Stevie has started to grow on me a little more as a person.

To everyone around, he is the outcast, the freak, he's obnoxious and he's wild, but when you get to know him, you actually see him for who he is and how kind he is to you despite all that has happened.

He could have easily snapped yesterday when they started to beat him. I didn't see it with my own eyes, but I heard what happened from Lauren, and she had to place all of her power on Donny's chest for him not to go after Brandon.

I will say it once and I will say it again, karma is a bitch. And Matilda, Brandon and their group of freaks will all be the ones who end up in jail, or single parents or living a life they wish they could escape from.

What goes around comes back around. But I am very proud of Stevie for not going after Brandon after he kicked him to the floor.

I also can't get over what he said to me, that I'm not as

invisible as I think I am.

That has to be one of the best compliments I've had in a long time.

School today was quiet, and although I wasn't purposefully looking for Stevie, I hadn't seen him around, so I'm assuming he was hanging with Lauren and Donny since I hadn't seen them either.

As I pull up to Stevie's house, he's already outside, waiting for me as I pull up the drive. Grabbing my books from my passenger seat, I get out of my car and make my way towards him.

He doesn't look up, only continues to stare at the ground. "Stevie?" I ask as I approach him. He slowly begins to lift his head to reveal the biggest black eye and bruised cheek I've ever seen. "Oh my god."

"Mom wants to go to the police." he says as he looks out onto the street. "I don't want her to."

I place my books closer to me as I join him at the step of his house. "I can understand that." I say, agreeing with him. "But she is your mom, she's going to be protective." I explain, which seems to make him laugh.

"Did you know she told me the night before I asked you to become my tutor that I was going to community college, and I had to give up my dreams so she can have some sort of normal child?" He explains, looking down and shaking his head. "I'm normal, just in my own way. What I like, other people might not like, but that doesn't matter."

"I know." I say leaning over. "Just because we don't understand you, doesn't mean other people don't."

He laughs, "Is this your way of making me feel better?"

"I mean it seems to be working, you're laughing." I smile as

Jolie

I stand up from the step and look down on him. "Come on, I get paid by the hour and I have some more questions for you today."

I open the door and I hear him follow quick behind, "Have you not answered a lot of your questions?" He says sarcastically as he shoves me slightly up the stairs.

"Believe it or not no. I have found more questions, and you are my little dicktionary. Therefore, you have all of my answers."

I watch him stop as we make our way down the corridor, "Don't say that again, just because I'm well educated, doesn't mean you get to speak about my dick."

I laugh. "Agreed, as long as you stop talking about your dick." I say placing the books on the desk and taking a seat.

"If you want it all you have to do is ask."

I roll my eyes. "In your dreams, Stevie."

"Oh, it happens." He teases me, which causes me to look up. "Huh?" I ask.

"I dream about it daily, if you must know."

He says it so casually like we are talking about our favorite foods that I begin to feel dizzy.

"Sorry, what was that?" I ask again.

"I dream about us, daily." He leans forward in his chair and grips the underneath of my seat to pull me closer.

"We can't..." I say softly as he places his hands on my legs.

"We aren't doing anything, until you're ready. And that is if you even want to do anything with me."

I struggle to find my words as I try and grasp what is going on. "I-"

"I know, you're not ready." He repeats like he did the other week. "But I know that you want this just as much as me, so when you stop being stubborn, we can get down to business." He says, letting go of my legs and leaning over to grab a textbook, but I stop his hands.

"Why do you play me like that?" I ask him honestly. "You flirt with me, get me horny and leave me high and dry. For someone who claims to be all about wanting woman to feel pleasured around him, you sure know how to make this virgin feel disappointed."

He stares blankly at me, "What did you just say to me?" He asks as he stands above me. Whether or not this is a game, this isn't a joke.

I stand to meet him. "You heard me, you talk the talk about being a man who puts woman's needs first, you claim you're a dominant, yet you crave consent, so how is it that when I'm telling you in a way that I only know how to express myself to tell you I want you, you throw me down again telling me that I'm not ready."

He doesn't say a word, only continues to stare down at me for a few moments, his face filled with confusion and lust that lingers with desire.

And when I feel his hands grab the side of my face and he inches closer, my body begins to feel that amount of need again. "Say that again." He asks against my lips, the smell of cologne and a small hint of tobacco hit my nostrils.

"I want you." I say breathlessly. And then it happens. My first ever kiss and fuck me it is breathtaking. Whatever ounce of oxygen I had left in my body is scooped up by Stevie and his tongue dancing in my mouth.

He grabs me tighter as we move in sync, this time I place my hands on his hips for balance as the more he kisses me the weaker I feel. "Fuck, this is better than any of my dreams." He

Jolie

says against my lips.

He releases his hands from my face as he lifts me up and carries me over to the bed, both desire, need and nerves linger in the air. And the nerves are mainly from me.

Our make out session lasts forever in a day until he decides to take off his shirt, revealing that beautiful new bruise as well as a hell of a lot of tattoos on his chest. I stare in awe, but also trying not to drool. Stevie isn't a skinny guy, and if he was allowed, he would have probably beaten Brandon yesterday or at least knocked him out with a single punch.

"Are you gawking, kinky?" he asks as he kneels over me smiling, almost admiring me.

"A little." I giggle, feeling his arm muscles and move my way down towards his stomach. "I can't help it."

He kisses me passionately, and it isn't filled with just lust but also care, and I can feel it in the way he holds me.

"Say it again." he repeats against my lips.

"Say what?"

"That you want me."

"I want you." I say again and I feel him deeper the kiss as he lies above me.

"Fuck, I wanted you since day one."

He begins to place my hands above my head, not in the sense of him restricting me, but more so, that he can take off my jumper. "If at any point you want me to stop, you tell me. Do you understand?"

"I understand." I say which causes him to continue to reveal my bra to him. I don't feel as though I need to cover up, because the second he sees me in possibly my most vulnerable state at this moment, he kisses me hard.

"You are so beautiful, Jolie." He says against my lips.

While our tongues dance in sync, we continue to take each other's clothes off, still not wanting to come up for air.

He slowly begins to move his hand down my stomach and to my lace panties. "I'm going to be gentle, but if it is too much, you need to tell me." He tells me.

"Yes…" I say almost as a whisper as he brings his middle finger up and begins to suck it, I watch, almost in shock that Stevie's finger is going to be inside of me at any second.

He leans down to kiss me gently, almost as a distraction. "You're a good girl, Jolie." he says to me as he moves my lace panties to the side. "You're going to take all of me, one way or another, do you understand?" He asks.

"Yes."

He kisses me hard this time, almost as a distraction as he puts his finger inside of me slowly. I gasp, and not because it hurts, but because it feels good. "You okay?" He asks to which I nod repeatedly not wanting him to stop. He ever so slowly moves his finger, and it begins to ease the need in between my legs.

"Fuck." I say breathlessly.

"Such a good girl." he praises. He very carefully picks up the pace, but still remains at the same rhythm so that it doesn't hurt too much.

It lasts for all of five minutes, before he removes his finger and looks at me. "If you're going to cum, you do it on my cock, or in my mouth." He says to me as he leans over to his dresser and pulls out what looks to be wipes. And as I look down, that's when I notice the little bit of blood. He is quick to grab my face to turn me away from it, using his other hand. "No one likes having sex the first time, Jolie. You bleed. But it doesn't matter. Because you're going to be the first girl ever who enjoyed having sex the night, she lost her virginity."

It wasn't even a conversation, it was a command, but although I feel somewhat disgusting and vile as I lie in a slight pool of my own blood, he quickly kisses me as he reaches back over to the dress to reveal a bottle and what looks to be a condom.

I watch, not saying a word as he removes his boxers and casually rolls on the condom.

I don't think his dick is going to fit in me, so I have no idea how he thinks all of it is going to fit. I stare almost in shock as I look up to him through my eye lashes.

"Lie back down baby, don't worry. You'll take it all like a good girl." He praises me again as he lies me down, pressing me harder into the mattress.

He pulls out the bottle and begins to put some of the contents onto his fingers. By the lack of smell, and how he begins to place it on both me and him, I've gathered its lube.

As he places it on my clit, I shiver at his touch while he massages it around still standing over me. "You're so beautiful, Jolie." He says as he leans down to kiss my lips before moving down to my neck.

He hovers over me slightly, placing his hand behind my neck forcing me to look at him. I move myself down, desperately needing him inside of me and he can sense this. "One second, baby, you'll not be this needy for the first few minutes it's in." He explains as he separates my legs and begins to carefully ease his cock into me.

I gasp, as I feel myself spread for him ever so slowly. It hurts, fuck it hurts, but at the same time, it feels so good.

"That's it." He says as he takes it out and slowly puts it back in but this time a little bit deeper, "Little bit deeper."

He does it one last time, and that is when I feel myself become completely relaxed as his cock settles in me. "Fuck…" I moan as he pushes that little but further in me and it begins to hurt.

He continues a little bit further before I place my hand on his chest. "Come on, Jolie a little bit deeper." He grabs the back of my neck forcing me to look up at him. "You can take all of me, can't you?"

It sounds like a challenge, but as I'm about to argue back, he kisses me passionately, and the way he is holding my neck with one hand, his other hand on my wait as he continues to enter me, I melt and that seems to let him enter me fully for the first time.

I gasp again from shock, "Stevie…" I almost cry before he takes my hair is his hand and forces me to look down.

"I'm so fucking deep in you Jolie, I could cum already, look at how you were made for me."

He places my head back on the pillow as he slowly begins to move within me. I whimper almost as he places his hands on the headboard to guide himself. His light whimpers and moans as he slowly continue to fuck me is exhilarating. "My body begins to relax, and the more I relax around him, it hurts so much less, and I want him to go faster.

"Please, Stevie," I beg. "Please fuck me."

He looks to me with a smile which changes the rhythm, so he hits me harder. "Such a slutty girl for me. Look at how you're begging. Do you want it harder?"

"Yes." I plead breathlessly.

"Fuck, Jolie. I'm going to cum if you look at me with those eyes again."

He continues to move at a faster pace pressing his forehead against mine as he lifts my right leg up to give him a better angle. We move in sync, breathing heavily as we both chase our release. He leans down, and kisses me, taking the oxygen out of my lungs, fucking me so hard the headboard begins to hit off the wall. The harder he fucks me, the harder I dig my nails into his back. He winces, but continues to fill me with every inch, whispering as he praises me.

Although he continues to fuck me, hitting my sweet spot every single time, I can still feel him being gentle with me considering it's my first time.

"Are you okay?" He asks against my lips, and he kisses me gently. I nod, not being able to say anything, even though I know he wants me to say so. But I'm chasing my release and I'm so *so* close. I close my eyes, focusing on the praises from Stevie and how he is hitting that sweet spot. Every. Single. Time. "That's it," He praises as I can feel my orgasm burn within me. "Cum for me." He growls, his tone so dark, that it does the job and I dig my nails into his back so hard, I'll be surprised if don't draw blood.

He holds me tight for a few moments while my orgasm escapes through me, as I open my eyes, I notice he's watching me. "What?" I breathe.

He smiles to me, "You're just so beautiful." He compliments me as he leans down to kiss me again, and I melt like butter in his arms.

For the next ten minutes, Stevie demands another two orgasms from me before chasing his own. "Fuck." He says as he whispers in my ear. Although there is a condom on, I can still feel his load within me, and it makes me feel better knowing that he finished too.

He raises his head slightly to reveal the sweat dripping off his forehead. Neither of us say anything for a moment, as he stares, breathlessly into my eyes. "Better than I imagined." He speaks after a while, following it with a wink.

I begin to feel my cheeks burn with both embarrassment and nervousness as I look away from him. He's quick to pull me back to him. "Don't ever look away from me, kinky. Understand?" He demands.

"Yes." I say, my cheeks are still burning. He leans down to brush his lips against mine.

"Good."

Stevie

I'm going to start charging Jolie rent for how much she's living in my brain rent free.

Yesterday has been on repeat since the minute I woke up and It's all I've been able to think about all day. I'm pleased there is no tests today, because I wouldn't pass a single one.

She was ever so awkward after, especially since I told her I was going to be cleaning her up. There wasn't too much blood, I thought there would have been more, but it didn't matter.

I knew she enjoyed it. And fuck I did too.

The way she moaned, the way she begged and the way she fit me perfectly is the only thing I've been able to think about since I opened my fucking eyes.

I've never had any of my previous sexual partners make me feel the way Jolie makes me feel.

Which has me worried.

Because I can feel myself falling for something that is destined to not exist. Jolie and I aren't people who should mix, and although sex is sex, yesterday was something deeper for both of us. It meant something even if she tried to deny it and if she feels as though it's all for research to her, and for me it's passing this test, I know how she kissed me. And you don't kiss someone you don't like, like that.

She kisses with passion, with her heart and it makes me ache for her more. No one in this world is like Jolie Mason. Because if the world knew of Jolie Mason no one would share her. And that's what I intend to do, keep her as close to me as possible.

I might be leaving in a few months for tour, but if I can convince her that when we leave this place I like to call hell, that she might even give me a chance one day if I deserve it.

But then it dawns on me, that the only reason I managed to get in this situation is because I blackmailed her into helping me. I want to kick myself, because maybe if I had approached her with a nicer tone, rather than expecting her to do something for me. She never had to do anything, but I was the one that treat her like shit.

I make my usual rounds, trying to avoid Brandon and Matilda so I don't get another beating like I did the other day. Lauren and Donny are still fucking like rabbits so I probably won't see him for the next hour, so I set out to find Jolie, even if it is just to pass her in the corridor and see her smile.

But when I approach the hallway, I don't see her, which is unusual. She's normally here at the same time, but she's not. And I feel myself begin to panic.

What if I took it too far last night, and she's taken the day off school? My mind begins to race with all of these different questions that I decide to just text her to see if she's in school.

Meet me at the old library. I text in in the hopes she answers to tell me she's here.

I head straight there, and as I make my way over to it, looking

Stevie

over my shoulder to see if anyone is following me. Obviously not.

I sit for what seems to feel like forever and then I hear the door to the front of the library open. And that is when I decide to hide, just in case it isn't her and someone else has decided to join me.

As I walk through the tall wooden bookcases until I get a better view of the door. I suddenly notice her long hair, one of her large baggy jumpers and mom jeans. Thank God, she's here.

"Stevie!" She calls out at me in an aggressive whisper. "Stevie!"

The further she walks away from the door, the quieter I move through the end of the bookcases, running through the one I know she wouldn't be able to see me go down so I can scare her.

She continues to walk forward slowly, looking out for me and as I quietly run behind her to frighten her, I begin to feel myself get excited as I reach for her waist.

She screams as I push her against one of the doors in the library. "Oh my god, Stevie! You frightened me!" She shouts to me, slightly hitting me while I begin to laugh uncontrollably. "Not funny." She begins to pout as I reach for her face.

"I'm sorry," I continue to giggle. "I'm sorry." I lean in, kissing her ever so slightly. I feel her place her soft delicate hands on my hips as she melts in my arms.

"You better be." She teases as she pulls away from the kiss. "Anyway, what do you need?" She asks looking up at me with those eyes. Those fuck me harder Stevie eyes and I suddenly feel my cock twitch with excitement as I remember her cries.

"I wanted to see you again." I tell her, which is the truth

whether or not she believes it, I still mean it.

"Mm," She mumbles as she leans back a little on the door. "I'm pleased you text me; I was studying, and I was bored." She smiles.

Fuck, that smile.

"Are you still bored?" I ask as I lean down to gently kiss her lips. "Want me to help?" I ask, to which she nods.

"Yeah, I mean I'm dying of boredom…" She trails off while I stick my tongue in her mouth to shut her up. As much as I like hearing her voice, I love listening to her moan more.

Moving both of her hands up to above her head, I restrain her there so I can have full control of her. She moans against my lips and although she doesn't tell me that she wants me to stop, the slight moans are encouraging me.

I reach for her pants, wanting to fully be immersed in her again like I was last night. "Stevie!" She gasps. I open my eyes to see a surprised look on her face. "We can't have sex here." She says which causes me to let go of her and place my hands back around her face, still wanting to be consumed by her.

"I thought public sex was something you wanted?" I tease causing her to giggle Mm before kissing her harder than I did before. I pull away after a moment, "Oh baby, is that what it is… are you sore?" I ask and I watch as her already rosy, red cheeks turn the bride shade of tomato, "Was I too rough last night?"

She continues to laugh as I place my hand on the door behind her. "You wish you were." She taunts which causes me by surprise.

"OH?" I ask with a devilish grin. "Was I too soft on you? Did you need to beg more?"

She nods, hinting she's playing along, but this just makes me harder. If she runs, I will chase her down. I don't even have a primal kink, but fuck me, I'd fuck her in public or in the woods if it meant I was close to her, our bodies touching and if she kisses me like she was to take my breath away. "What have I said, kinky?" I ask, reaching down to her pants as I watch her squirm.

"Use your words."

I nod. "And are you using your words, Jolie? Or are you being a brat?"

"Fuck me and find out if I can be a brat." I stand back, a look of shock on my face as I look at her, but I can't help but smile. "What?" She asks me, like what she's just said is in her normal vocabulary.

I continue to smile at her while my dick gets harder at the thought of her being tied up while I fucked her in ever position possible. "You're not gonna let me fuck you here, are you?" I ask and she shakes her head.

"Nope. I just wanted to make you so hard that you're struggling to cope." She grins.

I loudly exhale, both out of sexual frustration and general frustration.

"Well played kinky, well played." I smile back. "It's okay I can just get you back later when I get five orgasms out of you…" I tease as I lean in to kiss her, but she stops me.

"Actually…" She says as I back away. "I can't tutor you tonight." She says and I frown, sticking out my bottom lip a little.

"Why?" I whine and she tilts her head while pulling on the bottom of my shirt as if she's nervous to tell me.

"I have a family thing tonight."

"Are you just saying that to get out of tutoring me?" I ask, slightly narrowing my eyes.

"No, I have a family thing tonight." She repeats.

I continue to narrow my eyes at her before giving her a reassuring smile. "Okay." I say, leaning down to kiss the top of her head.

"I can tutor you tomorrow?" She asks and I smile to her.

"Sounds good. I will have to leave straight after as I have a gig in town with the band." Her eyes widen with curiosity.

"Well maybe I can drop you off?"

I smile. "I'd like that."

I do have to feel grateful for Jolie, because since she started to tutor me, she's only managed to move me up three grades in the past few weeks. I don't think she realizes how good she actually is. I just hope I don't fuck this up.

Jolie

Over the next few months, Stevie and I continue our routine.

We fuck, I tutor him, he tutors me, I leave. Simple and a nice arrangement.

He decided last Tuesday that this was the night that I got to see him dressed as Ghost from Call of Duty. And although I found it extremely attractive, it did creep me out because I felt as though I was having sex with a stranger. As a costume? Yes. Used for sex? Not a fan.

What makes matters even worse is that when we are together we can't keep our hands off each other. The little antic in the library a few months ago when he lured me out there just to scare me, kiss me and possibly use me for sex was when I realized that I am royally fucked when it comes to this situation.

I like Stevie. So goddamn much.

But I can't.

Although we only use each other to get what we want, it isn't healthy because we don't have anything in common, so if it was a relationship, it wouldn't work.

Stevie hasn't been the topic of as much bullying, and I have managed to avoid my parents and their hopes to lure me into some sort of agreement for months now.

Not that they care, they've been too busy planning this memorial trip for Isaac's anniversary next week. Something I'm dreading. A full week with no contact with anyone so I can do a trip my brother always wanted to do.

What makes it worse is they've planned it just before exam season starts and it couldn't come at a worst time. I don't want to go, and it isn't because I don't want to remember my brother, I do- it's the fact that they are acting like this entire week is going to be things that if we were asked to do it by anyone else, we wouldn't do it.

They hold onto the fact that he died like it is their only personality trait at this point. My parents used to be fun, but they lost all of their life when Isaac died, which is why they are so certain I'm not going off to college.

It's not as if they've given me a choice either, they are determined their only living, breathing child is not going off to a college thousands of miles away.

They've given me every single possibility that could happen. My plane could crash, I could get killed on campus, I could turn to drugs to deal with the stress. The list has been endless.

I can understand their concern, but they sometimes make me think that my life doesn't matter now that Isaac isn't here. And I don't think that's fair.

They want me to give up my life to get married, raise a family, to do a woman's role in this life to please her husband. I don't know where it all came from, because before Isaac's death, there wasn't any of this kind of talk. They wanted me to go to

Jolie

college, they wanted me to do what I wanted, when I wanted. I now just live in a box.

But even so, as much as I hide my life from my family I still love them. But I wish they would go to therapy (something they don't agree with), or just talk to anybody else about it other than me.

It's exhausting being in a family where you're invisible. And I think because I'm now invisible at school it shouldn't bother me as much. But it does because it's my parents.

As I pack my bag for my last day of school before we break up, I hear a knock at my door, and as I turn, I see my Mum leaning against the doorway.

"I thought maybe you could skip school today." She says softly. "So, we can go and see Isaac's grave together as a family."

I take a long deep breath. "Mom, I have a test today." I lie. "It counts towards my final grade; can we go after school?" I pull my bag on my shoulder and head to go past her but she stops me.

"No. You don't need your education Jolie. You need to start thinking about Isaac. About your family. You've gone on too long now thinking you can still continue your education."

"So, Isaac can get his high school diploma but I can't?" I ask, staring at her woman's.

"This is your brother we are talking about; you have to care for him."

"Mom, Isaac is gone!" I shout at her which seems to take her by surprise. "Isaac died two years ago, because he couldn't come home to tell you he was kicked out of the army."

That's when I feel it. The slap.

My cheek burns from the impact almost immediately as I turn to stare at my mother.

"You watch your tone with me, Jolie. Isaac died because he did drugs, they found drugs in his system, he was an addict. He killed himself because he hated coming home to you. Not us."

I push past her, completely ignoring her ridiculous accusation as I make my way to the front door. "Jolie?" Dad calls behind me as I run for my car. "Jolie!"

I pull off the driveway as I begin to make my way towards school, trying to stop my tears but I can't help but feel enraged.

Not only did my mom just slap me, but she blamed me for Isaac's death. She doesn't believe her parenting was the reason that he decided that he couldn't come home. She likes to paint herself as the perfect parent. But no parent would slap their child and them blame them for their other child's death. It's unheard of.

I find myself not focusing on where I'm going as I completely miss the turn off from school. I've never missed school until my brother died. But today, I don't feel like sitting for that period of time when I'm clearly upset.

As I drive in the direction of school, I see Stevie head towards it, and I put my breaks on to stop in the middle of the street. Making a U-turn, I head towards him, and he's noticed me, because he is standing there, watching me as I pull up to him.

"Jolie? What's wrong?" He asks as he leans down to the window. His face hardens when he realizes I'm crying. "What's wrong?" He demands this time.

"Can we miss school today?" I ask. His eyebrows raise, but not even a second later, he is in my car putting his seat belt on.

"Don't need to ask me twice!" he exclaims. "Where we going?"

I do another U-turn and head in my original direction. "Out of town, away from here."

Jolie

* * *

Stevie and I settle on a town a few over from where we live, and about thirty minutes away. He found a river, not far from the main town and we decide to grab a coffee while we sit and talk, and I divert the question every time he asks why I was crying.

"We going to talk about it?" He asks, causing me to look directly at him. He points to my face, and I move back almost alarmed. "The slight bruise is forming on your cheek, wanna tell me what happened this morning?" He continues to press.

I didn't think she slapped me so hard it had started to change color on my face. "Just an argument got out of hand." I say not wanting to tell Stevie too much, mainly because he doesn't need to know.

"Doesn't mean that violence was needed, so tell me."

I decide against my best efforts to keep Stevie out of this, I'm going to have to tell him because he will keep pressing. "It's almost Isaac's anniversary." I say and I watch the realization hit his face.

"Aah." He says after a moment. "Did you hit your mom back?"

I frown my brows. "How did you know it was my mom?

"You don't seem like the girl who suffers with Daddy issues."

I laugh, because I agree with him. My dad doesn't really bother all that much with me, not anymore. "She blamed me for Isaac killing himself."

His eyes widen for a second as he processes what I've just told him. "Wow." he says after a few moments.

"Yeah," I breathe. "But she will always blame everyone else for her own mistakes."

He only nods at me, looking out onto the river for a moment as we enjoy a moment of peace.

"My mom wants me to go to college and be normal." I find it hard not to laugh, because Stevie isn't normal, he never has been. "She did the same to my dad. She forced him to get a job that deep down, he hates."

I suddenly feel sad. Stevie's dad was just like him? To be fair, it makes sense. Because Stevie has always been different and always liked different music, different styles and his way of thinking. Now knowing he gets it from his dad, makes much more sense.

"Why did your mom want your dad to be normal?" I ask curiously.

He sighs. "I think it's because they were like us growing up. Complete opposites, and although she remembers loving him for who he was, how he dressed and how he acted, she also remembers the pain that came with it and how much dad was bullied because of it. I think she just wanted to put it in the past, and when she was ready to grow up, she told him he had to as well."

I sit and listen, not wanting to say too much. Stevie's life is drastically different to mine. Although my parents have good, great jobs even, Stevie's dad has provided a great career for himself even though it probably wasn't what he wanted to do.

"How did your mom feel when she seen that you were following in the footsteps of your dad?" I ask, but I can't help the worry that begins to fuel my body.

"Well, she tried changing me into someone normal, I tried out at football, basketball, hockey. It didn't matter, if I didn't my guitar in my hand, I wasn't doing it. I wasn't interested." I laugh at the thought of Stevie trying to catch a ball. As harsh as it sounds, he laughs with me.

"I couldn't imagine you playing sports." I giggle.

He scoffs. "I ended up tackled more than I did with the actual ball. It wasn't worth it, no matter how hard she tried to push me into it. I hated it." he begins to laugh. "She knew deep down I loved music. She just didn't want me ending up like my dad. I think she has a lot of bad memories."

I nod, agreeing. If they were like us, having a secret relationship because Stevie's dad was the outcast, it meant that she witnessed just as much heartache as I have already. Stevie being knocked down the other day was nothing compared to them getting him arrested.

"How did she feel about you getting arrested?"

He sighs for a moment. "Let's just say she knew that it wasn't me. It was something in my dad's eyes that told me that this wasn't anything to do with me and that night was because of some old vendetta Brandon's dad has against mine. He never said as much, but his face told a whole different story."

I instantly feel bad for Stevie, because he decided to be expressive with his fashion sense, music and personality that he is the target some decades old bullying that has been passed down to the next generation. It's sick.

"Well hopefully when we leave in a few months, it means you can focus going on tour and becoming your own person outside of this town." I say, trying to lighten the mood.

He smiles, taking my hand in his. "Exactly."

"So apart from Defending You Forever," I say wanting to change the subject. "What other bands do you listen to?"

"Well," he begins, "I love Metallica, Master of Puppets is my favorite. I've almost managed to learn it on the guitar."

"Really?" I ask.

He laughs at me, "Why are you surprised?"

"I don't know, it sounds hard."

"It is, but as long as you practice, it becomes easier." he smiles. "What about you? Who do you like listening to?"

I think for a moment. "Just anything that is on the radio, or on a playlist."

"Ah… so shit?"

I pull a face. "What's that meant to mean? I mean at least I listen to decent music unlike you."

"Err what is listen to *is* music, kinky."

I laugh. "If you say so."

"You seem like the type of girl to listen to sad music and watch Legally Blonde on repeat."

I move my head back in shock. "What gives you that assumption?"

"Oh! I'm not saying it's a bad thing!" he says trying to pull himself back out of the hole he has dug himself in. "I'm just saying it's the vibe you give off."

"Is there anything wrong with Legally Blonde?"

"No, Elle Woods is a icon, babe." He stands up, puts on his best Elle Woods face and looks at me. "What like it's hard?" He imitates, causing me to laugh so hard, I almost pee.

"How is it that you are just the most unusual man, but have seen the classic movies?"

"I can't be uncultured, Jolie," he says, sitting back down. "If I have kids one day, I'll have to educate them on it, and the more I learn now, the more I can show them later in life."

"So, you want kids?"

He laughs, like my question was funny. "Hell yeah I want kids. At least four."

My eyes widen. "Four?"

Jolie

"Yeah!" He smiles at me. "I can name them after my favorite rock stars." He says standing up, putting his hand up for me to join him. I reach out, grabbing his hand hard.

"What about if the woman you end up marrying doesn't want to name them Freddie or Prince?" I laugh.

"I'm sure I can talk you round." he teases, and I not only feel my heart stop, but my stomach fill with butterflies.

"Me?" I mutter.

"Yeah."

I stand, staring at him in shock. "Me?"

He rolls his eyes. "Yes, Jolie, you." He says softly, cupping my face gently as he stares into my eyes. "Because you are the first woman ever who has made me feel like it's okay to be who I am. While also showing me kindness, compassion and love when needed it."

I feel my heart ache knowing he is vulnerable as he says this too me. Stevie is always outspoken on his views, but when it comes to something personal, sometimes he cowers away.

"It's how everyone should be treat." I say in my defense.

"So, you're telling me, you don't feel the same way towards me as I do to you?"

I shake my head. "No, Stevie." I say quickly and I feel him begin to pull away from me, as I reach for his waist to pull him back. "you might have fell first, but I fell harder."

He smiles after a moment, and I can see the tear sparkle in his eyes. "Knew you would." He says as he leans down to kiss me. "I'm irresistible."

"Don't ruin the moment."

"Sorry."

* * *

Dealing With The Outcast

For the rest of the day, Stevie and I walk around this town, grabbing food, looking in stores and just all around enjoy each other's company. It was needed I think for both of us, and now that we are on our way home, I can't help but feel sad that this will be the last time I see him for a week. "What are you doing tonight?" He asks as we come through the town sign.

"Nothing, probably just avoid my parents, why?" I ask as I head through the town towards Stevie's house.

"My band is playing tonight at the old warehouse. Do you want to come?" He asks me, and I begin to smile.

"Finally get to see you on stage?" I ask with a smile.

"Yeah! What do you say?" He asks and I nod.

"I'll be there."

We don't say much more on the way home and after I drop him off and we say our goodbyes. I head towards my own house. It's not late, it's only five o'clock and the concert doesn't start till eight. But I can already tell that I'm going to end up in an argument with my parents when I walk through the door.

As I park up on the drive. I notice my mom almost hanging out of the window as I put the car in park. Jesus Christ.

I get out of the car and head towards the door and by the time I get there, she's already waiting for me, the tears in her eyes as she clings onto my dad. "Where have you been!" She cries to me. "We have been worried sick."

"What? Now you're worried about me?" I ask as I move past them. "Didn't think how slapping me across this face this morning was going to do to me?"

"She made a mistake, Jolie."

"So let her tell me that." I snap.

We both look to my mom who is crying uncontrollably. But continues to stay silent. "See, she doesn't care, dad. She doesn't care that she's left a bruise on my face." I say pointing at it.

"You blamed me for Isaac's death!" She shouts through her cries. "I was an amazing mother; I have done everything and more for you both."

"Was? Did you forget that after Isaac died, you still had to take care of the other child? Me!"

"You were fine on your own."

"Doesn't mean I didn't need you. Everyone grieves in a different way, mom, but you made it your entire personality, mine too!"

"We need to remember your brother."

"And we do! Every year we spend what feels like a month mourning him. I understand he was the favorite, everyone can see that. But stop trying to force me to do things that make me uncomfortable."

"It's how we choose to grieve."

"It's how *you* choose the grieve." I remind her. "No mother would force her other child to do everything the other sibling wanted to do. Forcing them to feel uncomfortable while we did everything he did. It's weird."

She wipes her eyes, and now that she seems to have gotten over the fact I left her this morning, her sadness turns to rage. "I knew that when you were born you were different. Growing up, although you were smart, and beautiful I knew one day you would disappoint me more than Isaac ever could. And today is that day."

I stare at her, the tears falling from my eyes. "If I'm so much of a disappointment, why do you keep me around?" I ask her.

She moves closer to me. "Because I can't have people think that we're a broken family while we mourn your brother. You may have been the reason he decided to kill himself, because he hated you so much, but he loved me. I am an amazing mother."

I narrow my eyes, although the tears don't stop falling. My dad stands there, not sure what to say for a moment. "What did you just say to her?" He asks my mother.

"Nothing dear. Jolie is leaving and going to her room until we leave for the trip in the morning, aren't you?" She growls to me. Hinting it's a command.

I shove past her and my dad, who I just end up ignoring. He's never really tried to be there for me. Neither has my mother.

But as soon as I'm out of sight, that's when I hear him defend me. "Our daughter isn't the reason Isaac killed himself, and you know it."

I stop dead in my tracks, wanting to hear my mom's response. "She's not my daughter anymore. She forced my son, to end his life." She repeats.

"No." Dad shouts at her. "You told him and I heard it, that if he didn't get into the army, he shouldn't bother coming back and he should kill himself. And because he was so scared of you. He did just that!"

"Richard, be careful how you speak to me." I hear her warn him. "I'll divorce you and take everything you've got, leaving you with that little brat."

I hear my dad scoff. "You've always been crazy. But this? It's a new level."

I decide I've heard enough.

I may not get on with my mom and I feel hurt how she would accuse me of such awful things when it has come to my brother, but nothing surprises me anymore.

Heading to my room, I place my bag on the bed and lie down next to it and softly begin to cry. Suddenly I hear footsteps coming up to my part of the house, and as I sit up, that's when

Jolie

I notice my dad.

"Hey." He says as he reaches the door.

"Hi." I wipe my tears with my jumper, wanting to just ignore what's just happened.

"Wanna go and get some ice cream?" he asks, which catches me by surprise. When I was little he always took me for ice cream after one of my classes, but he hasn't done it in years. I nod in agreement, wanting to get as far away as possible from my mom.

When we head down the stairs, I can hear her on the phone with one of her friends in the back room, crying about it. Dad and I make a break for the front door.

We run towards my car which is the one that is closest to the end of the drive and as we pull away, we both giggle like kids as we make our way towards the ice cream parlor, the only one in town.

We don't say much on the ride over, but when we get there and he orders us a Chocolate Deluxe Sunday, like we used to, it makes me feel a whole lot better.

"So, how's school?" He asks as we begin to dig in.

"I didn't go to school today." I tell him truthfully.

"Oh, I know." He smiles at me. "I got a call, just be pleased it wasn't your mom."

I press my lips together while also feeling grateful for him. "You didn't tell her?"

He shakes his head as he takes another big scoop of ice cream. "No. I heard the slap this morning. And when I asked her about it, the lack of care that she had for you made me realize that for the first time in a long time, I've let her go too far with how she treats you."

I narrow my eyes. "Dad? She's the devil."

He laughs. "Yeah. Since Isaac died, it's just got a lot worse. I blame the therapist. She once said that in order to move on and grieve you need the support of the town and your family. She ran with it, thinking that if she made Isaac's death her entire personality, people would sympathize. And they have. So, she's become unbearable."

I listen carefully. I didn't know that dad had took mom to therapy. However, it doesn't surprise me.

"Why do you let her treat me the way she does? You do know that I'm going to college right?" I ask him. "I'm not settling down and having kids and becoming a housewife."

He laughs. "Oh, I know. That's why I thought we could talk about college and where you've applied."

"Well, everywhere really. Some super far away, some closer to home. I really want to go to NYU."

He smiles. "Like your mom. She wanted to go there too."

I frown. "What happened?"

"She got pregnant with Isaac."

I nod. That makes sense. Mom was a year older than me when she had Isaac so she wouldn't have been able to go to college. "Do you think that's why she resents me so much? Because I am going off to college?"

Dad shrugs his shoulders. "I don't know, Jolie bear." He picks up another spoon full of ice cream. "So, tell me about this kid you're tutoring."

I smile. "His name is Stevie."

"Oh yeah? Do you like him?" Dad asks while giving me a funny look.

"Dunno what you're talking about."

"You like him." Dad teases, slightly kicking me under the table. "Your smiled when you said his name, that normally is a sign."

"Hmm." I say while taking another scoop of ice cream. "He's asked me to go to his concert tonight."

Dad's eyes widen. "So, are we going?"

I pull a face. "We?"

"Yeah. I want to avoid your mother, so how about I be the cool dad and come to your boyfriends' concert? Where is it?"

"It's at the old warehouse and he's not my boyfriend."

"Sounds like a plan." Dad smiles at me. "So, Stevie is in a band, huh?"

I nod. "They're going on tour in the summer with another band called Defending You Forever."

"Shut up!" Dad exclaims, almost dropping his spoon. "Your boyfriend is in Death Due?"

"SHH!" I tell him while looking around to notice the place is completely empty. "Yes, he's in Death Due and again, not my boyfriend."

"That is so cool. I love Death Due and the other band." Dad smiles, while doing a little dance. "So, why are you tutoring him if he is going on tour?"

I finish my scoop of ice cream. "As long as he passes the end of year exam, he can go on the tour. If he doesn't, he can't go. That's the agreement with his parents."

Dad nods. "Makes sense." He frowns. "Wait, which one of them went to jail?" Dad asks juts as I put another scoop of chocolate ice cream in my mouth.

"That would be Stevie."

Dad's eyes widen. "You're dating a rocker and a criminal. Fantastic. I'll expect teenage pregnancy too." He jokes as I reach over to shove him.

"Stop it." He begins to laugh. "When you were at school, did you ever know a John and Brandon's dad Theo?"

Dad pulls a face. "John the freak?" He asks and I narrow my eyes. "Sorry, John Pritchard and Theo Pogue. Yes, I knew them both. Not friendly but I knew them at least. John was a rocker, loved music and his band and really wanted to continue it. But we all knew who his wife was, and if she had any say on it, he was going to be giving up that lifestyle so she can do whatever she wanted."

"So, you're saying Stevie's mom was the reason why John had to give up his dream?" I ask, to which dad nods. It matches what Stevie said earlier today.

"Sure thing, kid. She was one of the popular girls in school who actually ended up falling for John we all left. It infuriated Theo. He wanted to marry her, but she didn't like him for how he treat John. So, she married John. Changed him into some man who if you passed him on the street you'd barely recognize him. It's sad really, but you do anything for the people you love." He says, looking down at the last little bit of ice cream. "You have it." He encourages. "Then I will have to clean your face like I did when you were seven because no matter how hard you try, you've ended up with ice cream at the end of your nose."

He hands me a napkin knowing I wouldn't let him do that. I giggle and wipe off the excess ice cream from my nose. "Thanks dad." I say with a smile.

"Don't worry kid," he stands from his chair. He's taller, and if you've ever seen Luke from Gilmore Girls, that's what my dad looks like. He has his own car shop and is always working on cars. Lives in a flannel and a baseball cap backwards. "Come on. I don't want to be late."

After the ice cream parlor, we head towards the concert, and

Jolie

I park the car.. This is where a lot of bands play these days, and it's a good place because the neighboring towns come here for the concerts too.

And because they wouldn't want to embarrass themselves, the popular kids stay away, because they knew they would be outnumbered if they decided to attack.

I never realized Death Due were so popular, but as we are heading in after giving our name at the door, there are hundreds of people beside us as we make our way to the stage, fifteen minutes before the show. "I'm so excited." Dad leans down to shout in my ear.

I begin to feel nervous. I've never seen Stevie perform before, and although I am excited, I'm also shaking like a leaf. I don't doubt he isn't a good performer, I mean they must be if Defending You Forever have asked them to open up for them on their tour.

Dad decides to get us some drinks before the show, I just ask for a soda and he decides to get a beer, since I'm driving. We decide to head towards the side and watch as more people begin to join the crowd. The excitement is a real as I notice some people from our school who you wouldn't even think are fans, are here.

The lights begin to go down, and the entire room begins to cheer.

Esther White is first to join the stage along with Sam and then Donny and lastly Stevie makes his appearance. Holding his red guitar as if his life depended on it. "Good evening everybody!" Sam says into his mic. "Nice to see you all back here. If you're new here, hi! We're Death Due. And in the summer we will be the opening act to Defending You Forever on their American tour!"

The crowd goes wild, and begins to chant Death Due, including my dad. "This first song is one our very own Stevie here has wrote, lets kick it off with a bang, shall we?!" The crowd cheers as the lights go down and the music begins to play. Stevie on bass guitar and vocals, sings his heart out while the crowd jump and spin around. The song is a mixture of both metal and rock, something I'm not really keen on, but my dad is loving it.

After a couple of their own songs, some new and some old. They decide to do a few covers. Dad is singing to every single one at the top of his lungs and I only know the Bon Jovi one and a song that I once heard in a movie.

"Next, on our list and this is Stevie's request." Sam says breathlessly into the mic, "is a song called Ultraviolet, not sure if you've heard of it?" The crowd begins to go wild, including me. Ultraviolet by the Stiff Dylans, from Angus, Thongs and Perfect Snogging the movie. A British movie, with the dreamy Aaron Taylor-Johnson.

"For a special girl who should be here tonight, I hope she is." Stevie says while looking around the crowd until he finally notices me. "Who loves all those shitty fucking movies." I laugh so hard. Little does everyone in this room know, he also loves those shitty fucking movies.

They start to play the song, and both dad and I sing at the top of our lungs. Dad liked the movie when we watched it together when I was younger. So, for him to know every single word, makes tonight even more special.

The concert goes on for at least another thirty minutes. And by the time that everyone starts to leave, dad and I stay in the hopes that he can meet Stevie.

I watch as he comes out of the back with a smile. "What did

Jolie

you think?" He asks as he pulls me in for a hug.

"It was great! Thank you for playing Ultraviolet." He laughs.

"I couldn't get the guys on board with Perfect Day from the start of the Legally Blonde movie." He teases.

"Stevie this is my dad, Richard." I say introducing him. Stevie sticks his hand out and dad greets him with a firm handshake.

"Nice to meet you Stevie, a big fan." He says with a smile.

"Really?" Stevie asks with a surprised look on his face. "Jolie, I like your dad already." He says pulling him in for a hug. Dad laughs, hugging Stevie tighter.

"Jolie, please keep him."

I roll my eyes. "Okay, you two behave. Stevie we will leave you to pack up. Come on, dad." I encourage. Stevie and I say our goodbyes and dad almost skips to the car.

"Ah! That is the most fun I've had in weeks." Dad says as we head on our journey home.

"It was nice." I say with a smile. "Thank you for coming with me."

It's been nice spending time with my dad. We used to do it quite a bit when I was a kid, but not so much now I'm grown and isolated.

"Thank you for letting me come." He grins. "Now your mother is going to ruin my mood." He exhales.

"It will be okay, we have each other."

He turns to me, a small smile on his face. "We do. No matter what."

As we arrive home, the lights are all off, hinting that mom has either gone to bed already since it's eleven o'clock, or she's gone out to a friends.

As we slowly and quietly open the door, we both realize that she is probably already in bed and decide to just head to bed ourselves since it's already late.

"Jolie." Dad whispers along the hallway as I head to my room. "We aren't going on this trip." He says with a small smile. "We're going to spend some time together. Just the two of us."

My heart does a happy dance. This has to be the best news, especially since my mom will try and manipulate my dad into going, I just hope he stays strong.

I pull out my phone and notice a text from Stevie.

I'm pleased you came with your dad. You looked like you were having fun.

I grin.

I had the best night. Thank you for inviting me.

I know you go on your trip tomorrow, but can I see you?

Smiling a little at the text, I decide to give him the good news.

Don't think we're going anymore, or at least me and dad aren't. He's telling her to go. And we're gonna spend some time together.

I watch as the little dots appear on the screen.

Oh. So, I came to your bedroom window for nothing then?

I jolt up and begin to look around and notice him standing on the garage above the house. "Stevie!" I shout at him while also in a whisper.

"I told you I wanted to see you." He whispers back. "So, here I am."

I run over to my door and shut it, hoping my parents can't hear.

He grabs my face as he pulls me in for a kiss. "You looked so good up there." I compliment him, and I feel him smile.

"Oh yeah?" he asks against my lips. "Did it turn you on?"

I kiss him harder, and I feel him cup my face more to deepen the kiss. "Yes." I say breathlessly against him.

Jolie

"Good. I just hope you're soaking."

He lies me down on the bed, as his tongue slides in my mouth and I grant him entrance. He begins to undo the button of my jeans and moving away my lace panties to feel how soaked I am.

"Such a good girl." He praises. Pulling away he reaches down to undo my shoelaces and take off my pants. I let him, probably because watching him perform turned me on so much I was going to be pleasuring myself away. "I need you to relax, okay?" He asks me as he pulls my panties to the floor.

He slides his tongue inside me, and I gasp at the sensation. "Fuck, Stevie."

Moving his tongue inside and out while lightly rubbing on the top of my clit sends waves of different sensations.

He glides one of his fingers in and I gasp, gripping the bed. "You're soaked baby." He says against me before continuing.

I feel my eyes roll to the back of my head as my release builds within me. He removes his tongue, and I can't help but whine.

He begins to move his finger along and just as I'm about to protest, he enters another finger. "Fuck." I whisper trying not to wake my parents. Rising from his knees he almost lies on top of me, fucking me with his fingers and I feel myself lose consciousness as I hold my breath.

Stevie grabs the back of my hair and forces me to look at him. "Cum for me baby, all over my fingers. Please baby." He whines.

That does it. I cum so hard I begin to see stars. He holds me tight as my orgasm shakes me, kissing me and whispering praises as he moves my hair out of my face.

"Wow." I say with a smile, and he joins in.

"You're a good girl aren't you."

I pull a face. "Only when I want to be."

He laughs as he moves a strand of hair out of my face. "Isn't that the truth." He removes his fingers and kisses me before grabbing a tissue off my desk.

Lifting myself up, I place my shorts on that sat on the bottom of my bed. "Nothing for you?" I ask as I wrap my arms around his waist.

"I have you. That's all I need."

Stevie

It's the last day of break before we head back to school. Jolie and I have spent as much time together as we can. Her mom ended up taking the trip on her own and Jolie and her dad have enjoyed their time together as a family. Her mom hasn't spoke to her or her dad since she left, so they don't really know what's going on.

We've sat and watched a movie and now, we are editing manuscript two hundred, cause every time she writes a sex scene, we need to act it out.

No complaints here, I'd fuck her until my last breath on this earth.

She's consumes every part of me, and while I sit here and admire her beauty, I can't help but notice a few freckles that are starting to appear on her nose. Jolie doesn't wear a lot of makeup, she's naturally pretty unlike the plastics that walk the school halls.

"So, what about if it was this position, would that mean it's better for both of them?" I hear her ask as I admire her face.

"What?" She asks, her eyes widen with fear. "Why are you looking at me like that?

"I love how red your cheeks go, even now when you ask me questions." I say with a grin. "Keep going, kinky." I encourage.

After a moment of silence, she does just that while I explain that every single position I've put her in for the last five months is what Daniel, her character, should be putting India in.

After ordering us some pizza, we decide to watch another movie before she has to head back home. Her mom should be back later tonight, and I know deep down she doesn't want to talk about it, it still pains me to know that she's nervous about going home.

I don't want her to feel like that when she's in her own house. I mean, I know she's applying to colleges, and as much as I don't want her to leave; I have to as well.

The tour is full steam ahead, I've signed the paperwork, so have my parents, reluctantly, and I'm starting to get my documents in order for each city.

We also met on a zoom call on Wednesday to talk about sort of set list and plans and straight after school finishes and I get that final grade, I'm going to be on the road for three months, and as much as I don't want to leave her. I'm so fucking excited.

I also feel guilty about not asking her to be my girlfriend. But I think we both know how we feel, yet we don't want to put a label on it. Just in case it ends up not happening.

She is who I want to be with for the rest of my life, and although I have to prove it to her, but showing her I'm not the same man that blackmailed her all those months ago, I also need to make sure I pass this test.

It's stupid that deep down my mind thinks she's going to walk away from all of this as soon as she got that piece of paper back, but my heart is telling me something different. That she wouldn't do that.

"I don't have to leave for another hour." She says as the end credits of the movie roll round. "What do you want to do?" I look down to her, hinting at exactly what I want to do. She rolls her eyes. "Other than me?"

I laugh as I climb on top of her and move her down the bed. "You're always on my to do list." I say lightly kissing her. "Any chance I'm on yours?"

"I mean, I can see if I can make room for you."

Laughing, I lean down to kiss her passionately which she grants with a moan. "I want to try something different tonight." I say against her lips. "Do you trust me?"

She nods as she kisses me, "Yes."

"Good."

I get off her and head over to the corner of my room to reveal a set of handcuffs, and a blindfold.

Her eyes wander as I place the items on the bed. "I want you to behave for me, be a good girl you get pleasured. If you're a brat. I'll punish you, understand?"

She rolls her eyes a little. "What if I don't want to be good?"

Fuck.

"Then I'm gonna make you beg until you tell me you can't take it anymore." She looks at me with her fuck me eyes, and all sense of reasoning with her goes out of the window. "Jolie, if you keep looking at me like that, I'm not just going to use you until you can't cope and are begging me to stop, I'm going to punish you until *I* say it's enough, is that what you want?"

She still looks at me with those pretty little eyes while she takes off my band T-shirt to reveal her very hard perky tits.

Fuck. Fuck. Fuck.

"Yes."

"Fuck." This time I say it out loud. I lift her up so she's standing for a moment, "Turn around." I demand.

Doing as she's told, I place her hands in the handcuffs behind her back and place the key in the drawer. "You're going to suck me off until your eyes water." I say in her ear as I feel her shiver beneath me.

I turn her around to face me while lightly forcing her to her knees. She looks into my eyes, never breaking eye contact as I remove my cock from my boxer shorts. She's only given me a handful of blowjobs over the last few months, and the reason being that if I let her do that, I'd get consumed with my own pleasure and I wouldn't pleasure her as much I want to. And listening to her moan while grabbing the sheet and screaming my name sends me completely and utterly insane.

I place the tip of my cock to her mouth, hinting I want her to open, and she does. While looking at me, she slowly begins to bob her head back and forth and the more I look at her, the harder I get. Those. Fucking. Eyes.

Moaning as she picks up the pace a little, I find myself whimpering as I normally do when she sucks my cock, because she does it so fucking good.

My whimpering encourages her, I know it does, because not only does she pick up the pace a little more, but she also begins to go deeper, taking almost all of me into her petite tiny mouth. "Fuck baby, like that." I say as I grab her hair telling her to continue at that exact same pace.

I know I shouldn't, and I should be punishing her, but she's such a good whore for me how can I tell her no? She moans against my cock as it hits the back of her throat, I'm struggling to keep my composure. I'm going to cum in her fucking mouth at this rate if I don't get myself under control.

I look down at her, and her pretty little eyes are focused on cock as she still continues to take as much of me as she can. Not all of it, and that isn't good enough.

Gripping her hair harder I move her head faster and watch as she begins to struggle to take all of me in her mouth.

She's gagging slightly, but I don't care as I force all of me into her mouth and hold it there. I release her and do it again. And again. And again. On the fourth time she looks up to me, her eyes watering as she stares directly at me. Fuck my life.

I release her and she begins to catch her breath for a moment. I kneel to her, grabbing her face. Worried I might have gone too far.

But then she smiles at me, and I can tell she enjoyed it. "My dirty fucking girl."

I help her up, kissing her passionately, not even caring that she tastes like me. If anything, it makes this experience with her more exciting. I turn her around, so her ass is in the air to me. It's so fucking attractive, and perfect. She's in black lace panties, just for me. She knows black lace is a weakness, and every time she wears it, I die a little more inside.

I caress her softly hearing her moan to the sensation. I slap it. Hearing her gasp as skin meets skin. "Count." I demand.

"One." I hear her say.

I do it again, this time harder.

She hisses. "Two."

I do it again, this time changing my angle to get a better hit. She cries, but I can hear the moan ever so slightly.

"Three."

I lift her up by her hair from the bed. "Are you going to be good?" I growl into her ear.

She giggles slightly. "What am I? A dog? Want me to bark too?"

Rage builds within me as I slap her ass again, harder this time. So hard that I can see my handprint on her ass.

"Say that again?" I ask as I slap her ass harder.

She cries out. "Stevie!"

"What did you just say to me?!" I shout at her.

"I'm sorry." She pleads from the bed. "I'm sorry!"

"Are you going to be good?" I ask again.

"Yes!" She screams as I slap her ass once more. "Yes!"

I turn her over, grabbing her neck firmly. "Next time you say something like that, I'm not going to stop."

I lean down and kiss her so hard that I forget to breathe and she's my only source of oxygen. I need to be inside of her soon. I need her to cum all over my cock so many times it's dripping.

Letting go of her, I fall to my knees and wrap my arms around her legs, holding her in place. She's bound and restricted. And fuck does she look good. I want to make her cum so hard she see's stars, just from my tongue and my fingers. Then I'm going to fuck her and fill her till she begs me to stop.

I move my tongue over her clit slowly at first but then I begin to pick up the pace. She's moaning and gasping as I hit that sweet gentle spot with my tongue, watching her try and squirm away from me. "Stevie," she moans. "Stevie please."

I know what she wants. She wants me to fuck her with my fingers. And I can understand why, because fuck me she looks hot as I feel her release on my fingers. And she tastes good too.

Sliding one finger in, her moans get louder as I begin to move inside of her at a quicker pace. She's panting and moaning, cursing me out that she wants more. I slide another finger in and she practically begs me to let her cum.

"Not yet." I tell her. "You'll cum when I tell you to."

She growls in frustration but continues to moan as I pick up the pace. "Stevie, please." She continues to beg. "Please, please let me cum."

I continue to go hard on her for a few more seconds before I can see her begin to cry. "Cum, Jolie. Now." I demand. And she does as she's told. All over my fingers and I know she's going to taste so sweet. As she begins to breathe normally I stand up and make her watch as I lick one of my fingers. "Mm, so good." I say to her before holding her head up to look at me as I glide the other finger that was just inside of her, into her mouth. "Taste yourself, Jolie. Don't you taste sweet?"

She nods as she licks all of her juices up. "Am I done?" She asks as I use my other hand to wipe the tears that have fallen."

"Not yet baby."

Turning her over and spanking her ass. I go into my drawer to grab a condom. Since meeting Jolie I've gone through eight boxes of condoms and if my parents found the boxes, they would think I'm some sort of sex pest. But it's what she does to me. I'm horny all the time just looking at her.

I roll the condom on nicely and place the wrapper to the side. Spreading her legs, a little more, I tease her a little as I glide my cock over her sensitive area knowing she will start begging for it like a good little slut.

And she does just that, moans and whimpers release from her mouth as I continue to tease her clit. "You going to take all of me?" I ask her and she nods, her head still on the bed. "Good girl."

I slowly glide myself in easily, since she is still so wet for me, and so tight. Cursing as I begin to move within her, her moans get louder as do the sound of the handcuffs. I want to take her out of them but at the same time, seeing her helpless and needy is sending me into a spiral.

Pulling her up slightly to choke her a little, my thrusts begin to get harder, deeper as I watch her tight little cunt open and take all of me. She's moaning ever so slightly and the more she moans, the harder I fuck her.

"Good girl, you're taking it like such a good girl." I praise her as I lightly lick her ear. She moans harder, and that's when I've realized I've found another weak spot.

I continue to fuck her in this position, as I feel her cum around my cock at least twice, the second time almost made me cum with how fucking hot it was.

I'm nowhere near done with her. But I can tell she's on the verge of breaking and I do remember I have to send her home to her father soon. As her third orgasm waves through her, I reach over and grab the keys and untie her for a moment, giving her a second to breath.

Releasing myself from her, I turn her over. Her mascara is smudged down her face and lightly you can see a small handprint where I have gone too far on her neck. It might bruise a little, but I'm sure it will be fine.

I need her to touch me, scratch me, bite me. I just need her hands on me. I place my cock at her entrance and slam into her again, causing her to almost let out a scream. I fuck her so hard she can barely keep herself together. She has another two orgasms in this position and fuck does she look good when she moans.

She grabs the back of my neck forcing me down to her as I continue to fuck her. "Please cum, Stevie. Please." She begs me.

Fuck. "Keep saying that."

"Please cum in me Stevie, fill me, please." She continues and that is what sends me over the edge. I cum in her, clutching onto her as my orgasm explodes within me.

Her begging me to cum is a new one. And my god I'm going to need her to do that again.

She holds me tight as I get my breathing under control. "You really know how to drive me crazy." I smile at her as I pull out.

I wipe her up first, completely ignoring the puddle of cum from her on my bed. Knowing I can make her feel like that puts a smile on my face.

Jolie puts my t-shirt back on as she makes her way over to the mirror. "Stevie!" She shouts at me as I make my way back from my bathroom with a new pair of boxer shorts on. "You've left a bruise!" She shouts, pointing to her neck.

As I head over to assess the situation, I turn her to look at me. She's mad, and I can understand why, I was way too rough with her today and that bruise, although quite low on her neck is going to need to be covered up.

"Hey," I say as I force her to look at me. "I'm sorry." I say to her.

"How am I meant to cover that?"

I hold her in my hands. "We will fix it, don't you worry." I kiss her forehead, as she sighs loudly.

"It's the last two months we have together." She says against my chest.

"How has this gone by so quick?"

"I don't know. But two more months and then I get my freedom." She says. As I pull her back to reveal the stupidest grin on her face.

"Oh yeah?"

"Yeah, so, you need to shut up and listen, so you pass this

test."

My eyebrows raise. "You know I'm going to pass this test because of you right?"

She grins a little. "Well yeah."

"Stop being a smart-ass."

Jolie laughs. "Sorry."

Not even twenty minutes later, I see Jolie off, waving at her as she pulls away from my drive and towards

After Jolie leaves, I get a text from Sam asking if the band can hang out at his place for a few hours. I decide to go since it's been a bit of a crazy week with Jolie and having a beer will be good.

* * *

I end up returning from Sam's a few hours later, not too late but giving myself enough time do have a decent amount of sleep before school starts again tomorrow.

Although I'm nervous to see the freaks, I'm also nervous to see Jolie. That bruise isn't great, so I'm hoping she can cover it maybe with a jumper, or a turtleneck. It's still cool outside so she will probably get away with it.

As I renter my room, It's more of a mess than it was when I left it. Granted I'm not a tidy person, but this is beyond messy. This looks ransacked.

Unless my parents have been in my room looking for something, I can't explain the mess. But they are both asleep so I can't ask them. Another late night for them at another work function, but this time for my dad.

I decide to get some sleep and just ask them in the morning.

Stevie

Because more than likely, they are looking for something that I just hope they didn't find.

Jolie

I managed to find a jumper that is going to cover this lovely new bruise that Stevie has added to my neck. My tight sage green jumper and my mom jeans are a nice outfit to wear, so I don't stick out today like a sore thumb.

Mom decided that she didn't want to come home after her trip, like she was meant to and has extended her trip. God knows why. Dad thinks that she's either made new friends or she's found someone new. Either way he's passed caring, he's been in talks with multiple divorce attorneys to see what the best way to go around this is.

He's thankful that they both signed a prenup before they got married all those years ago. He originally didn't want one, but he is thanking his lucky stars now that he was forced to sign one.

He also owns the house, meaning that he can legally ask her to leave. If she ever decides to come home, he will give her notice; he's not heartless, but he is also cautious of the kind of woman my mom is. So, he's hiring a really good lawyer.

Jolie

Parking my car in the school parking lot, I head into through the front doors. It's unusually quiet outside, which makes me feel nervous. Like I've forgot there is some sort of a meeting.

As I was through, I feel every single person in the hallway stare at me. I come to a standstill staring people down as they begin to whisper between themselves. I can't hear what they are saying but I don't like it. I don't like this at all.

I head round the corner to the main hallway to notice sheets and sheets of paper. On people's lockers, all over the floor, stuck to the door.

People begin to laugh as I stop in my tracks to look around and see what the hell is going on. A sheet of paper hits my feet and as I bend down to pick up up. My heart stops and I instantly feel sick. It's that page of my manuscript Stevie had.

"Here she is!" I hear Brandon say in front of me. I lift my head, trying to control my tears. I feel like I'm going to throw up. "Jolie the freak! You know, Stevie was happy enough to give us this in order to let him have some peace." I rise from the floor, the piece of paper in my hand. "How would your parents feel knowing that you write such disgusting stories?" He taunts, making some people in the hallway laugh. Almost half of the school is here, staring, laughing at me.

"I mean, who knew she was so disgusting in the head? We should have her sectioned, just like her brother should've been." Matilda laughs, along with her minions.

Across the hallway I notice Stevie who has finally made a grand entrance, his face is pale as he notices everything and what's going on.

The tears begin to fall down my face. "Stevie!" Brandon praises him. "Hey, thanks for inviting us after Jolie left last night. It was good to see what kind of filth she writes."

Stevie shoves him. "You broke into my fucking house?!"

Brandon laughs! "Slow down, brother. I don't know what you're talking about? You invited us in. Told us how you and Jolie have been sleeping together for months, how she is a vile, disgusting girl who is into some freaky shit—"

I decide I've heard enough and make a break for the nearest exit.

"Jolie!" I hear Stevie call after me. I ignore him, pushing past groups of people who begin to laugh at me. "Jolie!"

Continuing to ignore him, I head straight for my car. heading round to the driver's side and he runs past me to stop me from opening the door.

"I can't believe you." I say trying to push him away.

"Jolie you know I would have never given it to them."

I laugh. "Do I?" His face drops. "Stevie we had an agreement. You promised."

He takes me hands in his, "I never broke my end of the agreement. I promise you."

I shake my head, pulling my hands away. "I don't believe you." I cry. "And that hurts that I've just said that, but I don't."

"So, you don't trust that I wouldn't have ever given something so personal to the likes of Brandon and Matilda? Do you really think I'm that shallow?" He raises his voice.

"Maybe?" I blurt out. "Maybe you got what you wanted. A fuck buddy for a few months. Let's not forget how you got me into this arrangement Stevie. You blackmailed me. And now that we're only months away from this final exam, you've decided that this would be a good time to end everything."

"I would never do that." He says.

I shake my head, pushing him out of the way as I try to open my car door. "I trusted you. And now everyone knows."

Jolie

He moves this time, his eyes filled with tears as he moves watches me get in the car.

"So, what are you saying, we're over?"

"Yes!" I shout at him. "You think I'm gonna forgive you for ruining my life. I was invisible, and you made me visible and vulnerable to the entire world. I knew I shouldn't have trusted you Stevie. But that's what I get for trusting the freak."

As soon as I say those words my heart aches. I don't mean it. Even though I'm angry, he's not a freak to me. His face drops and I watch as the tears begin to fall down his face. "I know you don't mean that." He says as I slam the door. "Jolie get out of the car; you don't mean that."

I begin to sob as I start my car, pulling out of the parking lot and heading straight home. I shouldn't be driving in this state I should've walked, but the sooner I get home and am away from Stevie and the rest of my school, the sooner I can try and figure out what the fuck is going on.

Stevie is calling me on repeat, but I decide to turn my phone off as I make the trip back home. Mom still isn't back, but Dad has a meeting with a divorce attorney today, so he is going into work later.

Ten minutes later, I pull up on the drive, sobbing as I put my car into park and get out and head towards the door. "Jolie?" Dad says from the kitchen as he comes to the door to see what is going on. "Jolie, what's wrong?"

I run into my dad's arms, sobbing uncontrollably as he holds me tight. "He lied to me, dad." I sob. "He lied."

* * *

After getting me a hot chocolate and a blanket, dad ended up going to the school. I told him some of the truth, that I started writing a novel and it had some quite graphic sex scenes in, to which he cringed, but listened, nevertheless. I told him that I accidentally packed one of the scenes in my bag before school and that happened to be one of the mornings I was in a rush. Stevie was begging for me to become his tutor, and when the scene fell out of my bag, he decided to use it as blackmail in order to get me to tutor him.

Dad was furious obviously, and when I told him that Stevie had given it to Brandon Pogue and Matilda George and they had spread it throughout the entire school, he began rocking with anger. He wanted to get his hands on Stevie, but all I said was that I didn't want to talk about it and that I didn't want to go back to school.

He agreed and headed down to talk to the principal. It didn't go well, mainly because the principal couldn't give a damn and was quite happy to agree that I could do the rest of the school year from home apart from my final exam. I was happy with that. It seems that Dad is happy about it too.

When he got back, instead of doing any studying we ordered pizza and watched a movie. He didn't want me to be alone, because I was so upset, but also knew that I did need some sort of space, so he sat on the other couch.

When I eventually turned my phone back on, Lauren had text me asking if I was okay. She wasn't there this morning, but Donny told her what happened. She says that she doesn't know if she believes Stevie actually did it, and Donny sure as hell sure Stevie wouldn't do it. But I don't know if I trust him enough to believe him.

I feel terrible about what I said to Stevie, but I also miss him.

Jolie

And I know I shouldn't. Even if it had turned out that Stevie hadn't sent it around school, he wouldn't forgive me for what I said to him. I wouldn't forgive me either.

For the rest of the night, I head to my room, crying. The sooner I can leave for college the better. I've never had my heart broken before, but I sure as hell don't wish it on anyone.

Stevie

I haven't seen her in four weeks. I'm going insane. She's not been at school, she's not answering my calls and texts and when I tried to talk to her dad, he cursed me out. Telling me to get off his property of he will deal with me properly for breaking Jolie's heart. I don't even care about what she said, I just want to make sure she's okay.

About a week after the whole incident in the school, the bullying got worse for me and so far I've ended up the hospital twice. I've ended up with a concussion from them repeatedly banging my head off lockers, or off the floor. I've got bruises all over my face from repeatedly being beat. My mom is going insane. She's been to the police twice about it, but all they say is because I'm a freak, I deserve it.

Brandon and his little group of friends won't even admit that they lied. Everyone in the school thinks that in order for me to get back at Jolie, I ruined her life to make mine a little bit better. I don't know who would believe that shit, but by the amount of bruises on my body I would say that isn't the case.

Stevie

I've tried talking to Lauren, but she won't hear me out. All she's said is that Jolie is staying home for the rest of the school year, and that was mutually agreed between the school and her dad. What's even worse is that Lauren hasn't even bothered to go and check on her, she said she's sent her one text; which absolutely enrages me. If she could get her head out of licking Donny's ass for two minutes and actually check on her friend, that would be nice. It's not even for me, it's for Jolie.

It makes me feel sick knowing she's at home because she can't feel as though she can come into school. Not even a few days later, I overheard one of the art students say that Jolie's writing would make her read the book if she ever published it. Another student said that if Jolie is writing romance books, she shouldn't be judged for it. She should be praised. I just wish she was here to hear it.

I've barely been on my game for the past few weeks, and the band know this. We are so close to the tour that if I don't pass this exam in a few weeks time, I'm not going and this will all have been for nothing. Jolie will be leaving for college and I'll be stuck here trying to get into a community college. I've been trying to study, but it's no fucking use. She was the only one who could explain something and have me understand it. She is the only thing I can focus on right now and I need her to come back. Not just to help me pass the test but I need her in my life. Because I'm miserable without her.

Sitting in the corner of Sam's garage, I lightly play some chords on my guitar while we wait for Esther to turn up. "Stevie, come on man." Sam gets my attention. "I know you liked her and all, but it's been weeks. It's time to move on."

I shake my head. "I'm not gonna let her go this easy man. She means a hell of a lot more to me than anyone else. She's different, she cares about me."

Donny lights a cigarette. "You know, I'm not supposed to tell you this. But she's going to be moving to New York soon."

I shoot up out of my chair. "What?"

He nods, while taking a drag. "Yeah, she got into NYU. She starts early, I think a week after the exam."

My heart sinks. I feel both elated her for but also sad because she's leaving. "She really got into NYU?"

Donny nods again. "Yeah man."

"Wow." I sit back in my chair while I begin to process. "She really did it."

There is silence within the group for a moment. "Now you know that, are you gonna let her go?" Donny asks, handing his cigarette to Sam.

"Well I don't know if you can tell, but I'm hardly in a position to ask her to stay." I practically laugh. "I've not seen or spoken to her in over a month."

"So, win her back." Sam says like it's the easiest thing to do.

"And how to you think I should do that? She not even in school, she's leaving for NYU early, and she's not even left her house."

Sam shrugs. "Well how about we put our heads together and figure a way to get her back so you can get out of your miserable state and we can get back to being a band who is going on tour with Defending You Forever?"

I nod. I'll do anything at this point. I'm fucking desperate.

After Esther arrives, we all begin to think of ways on how I can get Jolie back. Some aren't half bad, but some are just outright stupid.

"Maybe, you can sing to her, or play one of her favorite songs through like a boom box."

Stevie

I glare at Donny, wondering how this man can understand Shakespeare, but can't tell that Jolie would absolutely lose her shit over that.

"If I wanted to lose a eye, I would put myself in the firing line of Brandon and the others."

Donny looks away, realizing that his idea is in fact, a silly one.

"Well you know how to do one thing." Esther pipes up and I give her a glare just like Donny's.

"Just the one thing?" I ask.

Esther rolls her eyes. "Well you managed to fuck up the only decent relationship you had, so consider this a compliment." She fires back. "You know how to write music." She says.

"Write her a song, man."

Thinking about it, it isn't a bad idea. I have been really down so all of the songs I've been writing are love songs and how much I miss her.

"Okay, and how would we perform it?"

There is silence for a moment while the rest of the group think. "What about the end of year football game?" Esther asks.

Donny and I shake our heads. "They want me dead Esther, what's to say they will let us perform at the end of year football game?"

"I know a way." Esther says with a devilish grin.

"I don't like that look." Sam says.

"Me either." Both Donny and I say in sync.

"You know that older guy I've been seeing?" She asks and we look around together before nodding. "It's the principle. I'm his sugar baby."

Our jaws drop in sync as we are all silent about this recent revelation. "Huh?" Sam says. And Esther laughs at us.

"Yes. I've been seeing the principle for the past nine months. And because he won't say no to me, he will let us perform." She grins.

A smile begins to grow on my face. "Isn't he married?"

Her smile meets mine. "Who said I was just fucking him?"

We scream. Some with excitement, some with shock. Who knew Esther got down and dirty with a couple? I mean it's not surprising, when we used to have sex she admitted she was into some unusual shit, but our sexual relationship didn't last as long since she started seeing this guy. Or shall I say, our principle.

"Moving on," Donny says after a second. "If you can write a song for her and we can perform it, it might make it a bit easier to get her back."

Everyone nods in agreement. "There is only one problem," Everyone turns to me, waiting to see what I'm going to say. "How the fuck do we get Jolie Mason to a football game?"

* * *

It's just days now before the exam, and our plan is in full swing. Esther convinced her boyfriend to let us perform on the day of the football game, and I've managed to get Lauren on board with my plan to win Jolie back. She was reluctant at first, calling me some interesting names to support her friend, but when I asked how Jolie is and if she's been to see her or offer her any other support, she quickly asked how she can help.

I've managed to avoid Brandon and Matilda for the last few days, mainly because I'm trying to not turn up to this football

Stevie

game with another black eye. I have my last few classes before this exam on Friday, and I couldn't be more nervous.

I've been studying too. Trying to remember how Jolie would teach me so I wouldn't fall behind. Once I had managed to get over the flashbacks of her smile and her laughter, I managed to focus quite well, quizzing myself almost daily on different topics. So far I'm getting 97% of the answers right.

That wouldn't have happened without Jolie. Her kindness, and her compassion while I understood each individual topic. The classes I chose weren't particularly hard, but it's because I didn't have a reason to learn, that was my biggest issue. And now I do, her.

Heading to my creative writing class, I sit in my usual spot. At the back, away from everyone. I've made it my mission to be at every single class, taking notes so that I can use what I've learned in the exam.

"Morning class." The teacher enters except this time, It's not Mr. Phillips. He's barely thirty, and dealing with us, whether it's poets, writers or musicians like me, he enjoys the variety. "I hope you have all managed to write your letter for today's class."

I lean down into my backpack to pick up my piece of paper. I wrote this when I couldn't write any more lyrics. It's about Jolie, obviously. Because she's all I can think about.

"Now I set both you guys and the other class that I have the same task. Write a letter about someone you care about and how they make you feel. And they went deep." The teacher smiles to us. "One I want to read out to you now."

I sit, nervously and hoping that this isn't Jolie's.

Her writing is something so special so if I do hear it, I'll know it's her in a heartbeat.

"This one was done by Jolie Mason." Fuck.

A handful of people turn to me, some smirking, but some give me a weak look as if they feel sorry for me already.

" Pain." The teacher begins. "All that I feel is pain. From the moment that I met him, all I could remember was how I hated him, how he made me feel. He used me because he wanted something. Used me and broke me and caused me pain. But it's my own fault for trusting him the way that I did in the end. Because when all was said and done, I was left with nothing. Only a shell of myself that I once was." Glares and some sorry looks begin to glance my way and although I can feel them, I still stare at our teacher, hanging off every single word. "His love has consumed me for this entire time. I sometimes lay awake at night wondering how everyone in the world got this man so wrong. He's nothing like what he has been made out to be. He's kind, he's compassionate, but he's also wild. All things that towards the end I admired about him. But the fear never went away. Deep down, I always thought he would ruin my life with a single piece of paper. Something that was once one of my deepest darkest secret, one day, it came to light. And my life? Well, it shattered. Not because I was no longer invisible, but because the person I trusted more than anyone in this world made me visible. Made me weak and exposed to the world I had worked so hard to hide from. This world is something that will kill all of us one day. Whether you take it from yourself, someone does it for you or you simply are at the end of your life, you'll always remember that one person and how even after everything, after you've tried to get over them, how you've tried to remember the bad things, the good always outweigh them. And you feel guilty for letting them go." The teacher pauses for a minute, while directing his eye contact at me. "I was once invisible to this world. It's how I liked it. But when I met him, he showed me that there is so much more to this world than hiding in the shadows. And for that I will be forever grateful. As for me? I'll be remembering the time that I spent with him. Laughing at his jokes or listening to his many stories. While also feeling guilty that I didn't keep my mouth shut that one day. He may have screwed me over, but he made me fall deeper than I will ever fall ever again. And to him, I am forever his. And he is forever mine."

I want to cry, sob almost. We both got each other so wrong from the beginning. We fell for each other.

"Stevie?" The teacher asks. "Would you like to read yours?"

I nod. Standing up. I know she won't hear this. But knowing that this will make me feel better some way or another.

"I have always been the freak." I begin my letter. "A freak that people have never tried to understand. When you're someone like me; people don't think you have feelings, or thoughts or that you're your own person. But then one day, someone comes into your life and shows you that it's okay to be weird and wonderful. Just because someone doesn't understand it and they show hatred towards you, doesn't mean that you should change to fit in. If we were all the same, then life would be pretty boring. And the day I met her, nothing was ever the same again. I never got to tell her that it's okay for what she said, or that it wasn't me that ruined her life. I wouldn't do that. The version of me she met all of those months ago was selfish and self-absorbed. But then when someone comes into your life and turns it around, you realize how much of your life you've lost being awful to so many people. You become grateful for the people that you surround yourself with, you notice people more." I take a breath for a moment, still staring at this piece of paper in my hand. "That one piece of paper ruined someone's life, never mind my own. I have spent my entire life searching for peace and for someone to understand me. And when I finally found her, she was taken away from me, just like my life was before. For a silly little mistake. I err- I don't blame her for how she feels. If anything, it shows she cared more for me that she thought. I fell first, but I knew she had fell harder, because her reaction showed me that. I'll spend my entire life making it up to her if she lets me." I smile at this last paragraph. "I once told her she wasn't as invisible to the world as she thought. And she told me I wasn't as weird. That's where our story should have started. But because I still held on to some of my fears myself. I let it all burn to the ground. I'll never stop fighting for her, because she's the kind of girl that once you fuck up once; she's not going to give you any more changes. And I knew that from day one."

I sit down, ignoring the stares from my peers.

Suddenly I hear clapping and as I look up to notice the teacher clapping, a few of my classmates start clapping as well.

"Fantastic Stevie." The teacher praises me. I sit back in my chair as the next person stands to read. I feel better for letting it out. But also, more determined now than ever to get my girl back.

* * *

After class, I decide to go and see Mr. Franks one last time. I don't have any more classes with him now and if it wasn't for him telling me I needed a tutor, I wouldn't have met or even spoken to Jolie.

Stevie

"Mr. Franks?" I say as I approach his door.

"Stevie!" He says with a smile. "Come in."

I enter his classroom and stand in front of his desk. "I wanted to come and say thank you." His eyes widen a little at me.

"What for?"

"Well, if you hadn't told me to get a tutor, I wouldn't have gone up a few grades and been able to take this exam. So, thank you."

He smiles at me. "Stevie, although I do not condone in the way that you convinced Jolie to tutor you, I'm also pleased you did. She needed someone like you in her life. She's such a sweet girl, but she wouldn't have stood up to her mom if you hadn't made her realize how bad her mom was."

"Is it still bad?" I ask curiously.

"Well, that is a conversation for you both to have, but I will say that Richard is getting a divorce, he's keeping the house and Jolie. So, there is a plus to this."

I smile knowing that this is probably best for them. I don't know what's happened with her mom, but, I know Jolie needed her dad. He seems like a great man.

"I was wondering if you can do me a favor?" I ask and he looks up at me.

"What is it, Stevie?"

"Well in order to win Jolie back, I need her dad on board. Could you put in a good word for me?" I ask nicely.

He smiles at me. "Although Richard is my friend, you also have surprised me Stevie. I'll put in that good word, but it will be the only one. I just hope you have a good plan to get her back."

I smile to him. "I just hope I can convince her father to get on board."

As I make my way back to the door, he calls my name. "Stevie," I turn to him. "Is what you're going to do, gonna land you back in jail?"

Laughing, I shake my head. "No, sir."

He takes a long deep breath. "Thank god." I continue to laugh at him a little. I don't blame him for thinking the worst, I can be pretty unpredictable.

"Thanks a bunch, Mr. Franks."

"Good luck, Stevie. Do me proud."

Jolie

It's exam day. And I'm nervous as hell.

I've avoided everyone from school for the past eight weeks, and although I deep down believe that people have probably forgotten about the whole thing, with me actually doing the exam in the same hall as the other students, it's going to cause a stir again.

I've not seen or spoken to Stevie since then. Mainly out of guilt. Although he hurt me by doing something I should never forgive him for, I've still been worried about him and if he is going to pass this exam. It worries me.

This final exam means everything. It means I get my full scholarship to NYU; it means support, it means so much. I have to nail this exam. No distractions, just focus. *Focus Jolie.*

After parking my car at the community hall, I make my way over, ignoring some rude stares that are in my direction. I'm trying to focus on anything but them, but it's hard when the last time that you see them was the day your life was turned upside down.

As much as I want to run away as I'm out of my comfort zone, this is my only chance, and I'm not ruining it. Not for some people who decide to judge others.

I sign in at the desk and head straight to my seat. Row M, seat six. I begin to get myself comfortable for the exam, still avoiding all of the eyes on me. When I eventually look up and notice other people heading to their seat, that's when I notice Stevie for the first time in eight weeks.

His hair is still the same as it was, mid-length, straight and his tattoos are on show. He's wearing his usual attire, black skinny jeans paired with a plain black t-shirt with slight holes in. The classic Stevie style. He smiles ever so slightly at me, before giving me a wink and taking his seat, not bothering to look back over.

The last few people sign in and take their seats, and before we all know it, the test has begun, and our lives are about to be changed forever.

* * *

Once the test is finished and I hand in my paper, I head straight home, not wanting to join in any awkward conversations. I'm also avoiding Stevie and although the smile he gave me was slightly reassuring, I have my life to think about now. I'm just really hoping that he's passed.

The school's football game is tonight, and as much as Lauren has been trying to get me to go, I really don't feel like it. The last time I was surrounded with these people before today was when they all laughed at me instead of realizing that I was the victim. If it was them, they wouldn't have liked it, but because

Jolie

it was the quiet girl with trauma already, they didn't seem to mind laughing.

"I'm home!" I shout through the house as I walk through. Dad served mom with divorce papers about three weeks ago. The only thing that he has heard from her since her trip is that she's going to take him for everything he has. But he's said the house is in his name, they don't share finances, and they don't have a lot of things that are shared, that the only thing mom can use against him, is me. And she hates me, so I doubt she will want to try and get full custody. Besides, I'm heading to college and dad is paying a lot of it, especially since it's in New York.

"How did it go?" Dad asks as he approaches me from the kitchen.

"Good, I think." I hug him. "Let's just hope I pass" He pulls away after a moment, and that is when I notice the smell. "What is that?" I ask as I sniff his clothing. "Is that chocolate?"

I practically run to the kitchen to see a chocolate cake with the writing "happy last day!" I smile like a kid on Christmas.

"I'm so proud of you, Jolie." Dad smiles back. "You've made me proud these past few months, not just with how you've handled everything, but how you've managed to keep me sane while I'm going through this divorce." He pulls me in for a tight hug. "I was a terrible father to you, Jolie." he begins to get upset. "I'm so sorry."

I pull him in for a tighter hug. "Don't be sorry, we both didn't want to upset her." I feel him lightly cry on my shoulder. "We found each other again and that is all that matters."

We stay like this for a short while, just enjoying the moment. He eventually pulls away from me, wiping his eyes as he looks down at the cake. "In all honesty, I doubt this is edible, I made it after you left for the exam, and I nearly burnt the house down."

I can't help but laugh. I needed a good giggle. "Don't worry, I'm just pleased you're okay."

He takes my hand in his. "I'm always okay when I'm with you, kid." After a few short moments, I head over and pick up two forks so we can dig in. "Sure, you want to try it? It's probably terrible?"

I laugh once again. "Well, we have to try it and find out now don't we?"

He laughs along with me and take a bite with me. Staring directly at each other, we both pull the same face as we begin to eat the cake. "You know, I think I might have put salt rather than sugar in this." He laughs while running to the sink as he spits out the cake. "Oh my god that's disgusting."

I open the bin to spit mine out. "I think we can tick baker off the list of thing's you're not ever allowed to do again."

He nods while grabbing both of us a bottle of water out of the fridge, you can say that again." We both begin to laugh hysterically at the situation, but I can't help but feel grateful for my dad. In the space of a few short years, he lost his son, his wife and now he realized he can't bake. It's a very sad time for him.

"How about we go and get ice cream instead?" I request as I push the cake into the middle of the counter.

"We could… or…" he begins to say, causing me to look around. "We can go to your schools football game tonight?"

I heavily roll my eyes. "Not you too!" I shout as I begin to make my way through the corridor and up the stairs.

"Come on Jolie bear! It will be fun, promise. And straight after we can get some ice cream."

I stop on the stairs and glare my eyes. "Fine, but if you

Jolie

overhear anything nasty being said about me, you have to punch anyone and everyone, do you understand?"

He smiles. "I will go to jail for you, have I not made this clear?"

I roll my eyes again and continue to head up the stairs. "Whatever, dad."

"We leave in two hours!"

I can understand why he wants to leave early. There will be a fair on, we can get some food and he will want to see whatever band they have performing. It's the same every single year.

Even still it will be fun for us to get out and do things together. I decide to text Lauren to let her know that I'll be attending after all, so I will see her there. She almost instantaneously messages me back. "You have no idea how excited I am for this!" Although I'm curious as to what she means, I decide just to ask her when we meet up later.

For the next two hours, I decide to get dressed and make myself look presentable and happy. I really don't want to go tonight, but my dad loves going to these sorts of events so I can't exactly say no to him when I will be leaving in a week.

I decide to drive in the end after a few disagreements, and once we make it to school, I park in the nearest spot I can. It's already busy, as in super busy. Dad gives me a reassuring hug that everything is going to be okay, and that he isn't going to let one person say one bad thing about me. Deep down, I doubt they will. Especially since I'm with him.

Over the next hour, dad and I play some games, get some food and have a good laugh. I completely ignore the stares. I'm leaving soon, I'm leaving this town. The only thing I will come back for is to visit my brother's grave. I don't need to be back here for anything else.

Leaving my dad to try and win me a teddy bear, I head for a bathroom. The game is starting soon, and I'd rather just get through it so this is over and done with.

As I head into one of the stalls, ignoring some stares from some girls in my year group. If they wanted to say something they would've. So, I'm grateful that so far no one has bothered to say anything or approach me.

"Did you hear?" A familiar squeaky voice that I can instantly tell is Elle, says to someone else who enters the bathroom. "Jolie Mason actually turned up."

I hear another girl laugh and by how sinister it is, I can instantly tell its Matilda. "She's got some nerve. I thought we got rid of her two months ago."

"Well, she had to take the exam…"

"I don't care." Matilda snaps. "I thought we dealt with it when Brandon broke into Stevie's house. I mean finding that bit of paper that was Jolie's was just what we needed to break Stevie in two."

My heart sinks. Stevie was telling the truth. "Don't you feel bad? I mean, Jolie really didn't do anything wrong…" Ellie says coming to my defense. I'll never agree with the popular on anything, but I agree with Elle on this.

"Jolie Mason made the mistake of coming back to my school after her brother died. She took all of the attention off me for about a month. Do I feel bad for her? No. Because she got what she deserved. So, I'm happy about it. Both Stevie and Jolie are miserable."

I feel rage build within me. Both Brandon and Matilda had a vendetta against Stevie and I. All because of public image and popularity.

Flushing the toilet, I open the stall door. Elle's face drops as

Jolie

she moves away from Matilda, almost as if she's embarrassed to be seen with her.

"Don't you feel guilty?" I ask as I begin to wash my hands, feeling both her and Elle staring at me.

"No." She giggles. "Should I?"

"You should. Because you wouldn't like it if this happened to you."

She scoffs. "No one would ever do this to me. I'm not a freak like you."

I head over to grab a paper towel to dry my hands. Matilda is the same height as me, so I wouldn't be too worried about standing up to her. Walking over to her, I see her ever so slightly back away. "One day Matilda, you're going to get what you deserve. Karma is a bitch and it always comes back round."

You can see some sort of fear in her eyes. "Are you threatening me?"

I laugh in her face. "No. I'm warning you. There is a difference which you probably can't understand. So let me make this crystal clear —"

She backs away from me a little more as I stand a little closer. "If I ever hear that Brandon and one of his little freaks has touched Stevie, I'll deal with you personally. First your hair extensions, then your false eyelashes, then all of your plastic surgery. Cause to me, you've never been pretty, even with the extra help."

She begins to shake ever so slightly. "That sounds like a threat."

"So, make sure that your little boyfriend listens, cause if you want to not end up being the freak in this town. You may want to listen to me. After all, Stevie taught me well."

I shove past her, and I can hear her ever so slightly begin to freak out as I walk down the hallway, a smile on my face. I've always wanted to stand up to her, and now that I have, it feels so fucking good.

I'll need to find Stevie, and I'm hoping that I do before the end of the night. I need to plead for forgiveness, I just don't understand how I didn't see it before? I knew deep down it wasn't him, and with the outburst at the school to Brandon, it was clear, at least to other people maybe that he didn't have any part in this. I have so much making up to do.

Stevie

I think I've been staring at this text from Lauren for the past five minutes at least. She's coming. Jolie is actually going to be at the football game.

I really do owe her dad and the agreement after coffee and a good talk is that as long as I get him a ticket to every single Defending You Forever and Death Due concert when they're in New York, he will help me no matter what. He also said he will break my face much worse than the other kids will have if I break Jolie's heart again. Which I can understand. He also understood where I was coming from too and when I explained that on the security camera at the house you can see three males enter through my bedroom window just ten minutes after I left to go to Sam's for a beer.

Mom wants to press charges, and I don't blame her, I will eventually. But I just need to find the right time and the right amount of dirt on Brandon, if any at all. The security system isn't great, so you can't exactly see all of their face. But it doesn't matter, I just hope I can win her back with this song.

Dealing With The Outcast

A mixture of the Stiff Dylans, One Direction, who she loves but would never admit, and a bit of Bon Jovi. Something unusual and different but defiantly something fun. We've checked the kit over and over again and everything is there. So, all we need now is for people to take a seat and for us to be announced.

People begin to fill the stalls and as much as the stadium isn't gigantic, it's the biggest space that we've performed in, and nerves are high.

I've heard from Donny that Jolie is here, so I think that is why my nerves are shattered. Not because I'm about to perform in front of thousands of people, but because the girl I love more than anything is here and I'm going to win her back. I have to win her back.

The last few people begin to join in the stands, and we watch as Esther's boyfriend, the principle, begins to head to the middle of the stage. "Good evening everyone!" He shouts through the mic.

The crowd cheers, and we all begin to look at each other, nervous about what is about to happen. "We have a great evening ahead of us! We have a performance from our very own Death Due who will be performing with Defending You Forever over the summer."

The crowd goes wild, Sam managed to secretly get people from neighboring towns to attend just in case things went a bit south. We have fans from this town too, just when you have over three hundred people turning up from different places, it defiantly puts your mind at ease a little.

Brandon won't be able to come near me, and neither will any of his little minions. He wouldn't do it in public, where there is police, not that they would care, they would watch it happen,

Stevie

and where all the parents of the other kids are. It would cause a riot, or at least I hope it would.

I can't see her yet, but from where I'm standing, I can't see a lot, only the stage. I had asked her dad to try and sit in front of the stage so I can see her when I'm singing.

This song is my entire soul, it's everything I feel for Jolie and more. I think what makes me more nervous about it is that I'm singing it, not Sam.

"So please welcome to the stage, Death Due!" The principle cheers. We can hear a couple of boos as we head out to the stage, but they are almost completely silenced by the cheers. I continue to look out for her but can't see her yet and I begin to feel nervous. Lauren said she'd be here, where is she?

We begin to get set up, and as Sam is about to speak into the mic, he looks over to me with a smile and it tells me everything I need to know. She's here.

I follow his eyes until I see her. Her dark brown hair is sitting perfectly on her shoulders, even from here I can tell she got dressed up, and fuck does she look good. She's not dressed in her usual jeans and a jumper, but rather a tight black plain t-shirt, a brown jacket and what looks to be black tight pants. She looks incredible.

She gleams at me, and I feel my heart ache for her. She's smiling at me, that has to be a good sign. "We are Death Due." Sam says into the mic and the crowd goes wild. "If you haven't heard of us, don't worry; we're going to be singing songs that most of you will know, so if you know the lyrics please join in." he encourages the crowd before looking over at me. "But first, Stevie, our bass guitarist has something to say... or rather sing."

Sam moves out of the way to give me some room to the front

of the stage, I stand there, not bothering to stare at anyone else other than Jolie and her beauty. "Hello." I clear my voice. "My name is Stevie Pritchard, but if you've gone to this school long enough you will have called me Stevie the freak, and that's okay." I decide to break away from Jolie for a moment as I look out onto the crowd. "For years in this tiny little town I've been made out to be the villain in all of your stories. But, if you had got to know me, you would have realized that I was just misunderstood." I look back to my band members. "These people on this stage encouraged me to be who I am today, no questions asked. And for them I'm eternally grateful." Cheers begin to form on the stands as Donny and Sam both place their hands on either side of my shoulders. "My parents, although worried about me all the time, always have encouraged me to be who I am." I find my parents in stands, giving them a wave. I didn't think they would actually turn up, especially my mom who doesn't particularly like this sort of music. "But lastly there is one person in this stadium who told me that it's okay to be different, because if we were all the same the world would be boring." I lock my eyes back at Jolie, "And as much as she tried to hide from this world, she was never invisible to me. And I dedicate this song, and my success to her."

Sam hands me my guitar, picking up his own in the process.

Esther begins to play on the drums and my band, and I begin the song. A mix of pop and rock to start the crowd of strong.

Smiling at Jolie, I begin to sing, pouring my entire heart into this song that is for her and her only. As the chorus hits, the crowd cheers and begins to stand up from their seats to dance, cheer and join in. As the next part of the song goes ahead the next few lyrics are about Jolie and Jolie only.

"But when I met her she was shy and didn't seem to pry.

Stevie

But then I found out romance was her thing, and my brain went dingaling!" I watch as Jolie begins to laugh, a little from embarrassment but more with happiness and my heart begins to do a happy dance. "But guess what?" "What?" Esther says into the mic behind me.

"Well, she's a smutty book writer and you're damn right I kinda like her!" The crowd cheers as I watch Jolie continue to laugh and cheer. Her dad joins in which makes my smile like a fucking idiot to the crowd.

The song eventually comes to a close and the band and I stand for a moment watching almost the entire stadium cheer for us. My heart is full, and as I move my eyes through the crowd past my parents back to Jolie. She's smiling and cheering me on. The more I look at her, the more I realized I had been the biggest fool for letting her get in the car that day. I should have talked it out with her, but this? At this moment, nothing can be better than this.

For the next fifteen minutes, the band and I perform two of our own songs as well as some fan favorites to get people excited for the game. I couldn't give a shit about football, and once my guitar and

the band kit has been put away, I'm going to find my girl, who will no doubt be in the stands with her dad.

We decide to put our things away first and get it over with. Donny and Lauren will be heading to their usual hang out, Esther is going home cause she hates football and only performed at this for me, and Sam has a new side chick who he's seeing, so no doubt he will be heading to see her.

The game kicks off a few moments later, and as we begin to put our stuff into the van, I feel my phone buzz in my denim jacket pocket, and when I pull it out to see who's it's from, I begin to get butterflies when I notice the text is from Jolie.

"Hey rock star. Meet me at the old library."

Saying goodbye to my band, I head straight in that direction, not wasting a single breath as I run towards her. Please be here, please be here. As I open the door and see the room empty, I can't help but instantly feel my heart begin to ache. She wouldn't have set me up would she?

Just as I begin to turn around, I hear the door behind me slam and I almost jump out of my skin. There she stands, looking as gorgeous as ever. "Hi." she says after a moment.

"Hi." We both stare at each other, realizing neither one of us knows what to say. "You look good." I blurt out, because my god does she. Her body is so fucking good and although I'm jealous that she's wearing it out, I'm also grateful she's wearing it at all.

"So do you." She compliments me and I feel my heart do a thousand back flips. "I'm sorry for what I said," she says as she begins to break the space between us. "I really didn't mean it."

"I'm sorry too." I say walking towards her. "I should've trusted you, I should've given you the piece of paper back. It's my fault they found it."

She places her hand over my mouth to stop me from talking. "I don't blame you, for what they did. In fact, I don't blame you at all." She smiles through her tears. "I should be the one begging for forgiveness, because I clearly didn't trust you. I should've known that Matilda and Brandon were behind it all. I should've trusted you, because towards the end you gave me every reason to."

She removes her hand from my mouth and takes my hand instead. "Are you done talking so I can kiss you now?" I ask as she looks up to me. I remove my hand from hers and place

Stevie

both of my hands on the side of her head, wiping away the tears that fall from her eyes to her cheeks. "I will always forgive you, Jolie Mason." I say against her lips. "You are forever mine, and I am forever yours."

I kiss her first, and the sparks between us begin to fly throughout the room. I love her with every part of me. And I will never let anyone make me feel guilty for being in love again.

"You want to know what makes this even funnier?" She asks as she pulls away.

"What's that, kinky?" I smile down at her.

"We don't get our exam results till after the tour starts. So, you're parents are gonna have to let you go on this tour no matter what."

I press my lips together, trying not to laugh at the situation. "How did I not know that the results come out after?"

She giggles. "I don't know, but hopefully your mom can be convinced?" She asks.

I nod. "Let's hope so too. Otherwise, I'm screwed."

I lean down to kiss her again, and she pulls away. "I liked the song." she grins at me. "But it's going to have to have a name change because I can't have the world know I write smutty stories."

I remove my hands from her face and take her hands instead. "You know, I think Smutty Book Writer is a very fitting name for a girl like you. It was either that or the virgin Jolie so I thought I would go with the first one."

She moves away, lightly hitting me on the arm as she begins to laugh. "You're a freak, Stevie." She giggles, and I begin to join in.

"Only for you. But let's not forget, that you, Jolie Mason may look vanilla. But underneath your sweet girl persona is a freak in the sheets." I pull her close, smashing my lips to hers as I lift her up so I can hold her. This is everything I wanted and more, she is everything I wanted and more.

Who knew that a wannabe rock star and a smutty book writer would end up falling in love? But hey, stranger things have happened.

Epilogue

Jolie

Ten Years Later...

"It is not time to get out of bed yet!" I shout out as I hear small giggles around me. It suddenly goes deathly silent in the room, and I begin to feel nervous, because when they are quiet, it normally means trouble. However, I can say the same for Stevie.

Just as I'm about the remove the covers from over me, giggles and tickles consume the air and I laugh uncontrollably as I begin to be tortured. It doesn't last longer than a minute, but once the covers are removed from my face, I am greeted with three smiling faces, two of which I produced myself.

After high school, Stevie went on tour with his band Death Due for the summer as the opening act to worldwide sensation, Defending You Forever. They gained some serious traffic on social media, and before the band knew it, they became an overnight sensation.

In the last ten years, Stevie has been on multiple tours with the band, started slightly heading off into a solo career himself with his debut single, Yours Forever hitting the Billboard Top 100, staying very strongly at the number two spot for twenty-seven weeks.

But never once did he forget about me or make me feel like I wasn't important.

I went on to do my creative writing degree at Columbia University and although I loved every minute of my time there, I was so excited to move somewhere new.

I always thought New York would be for me, but it turns out, I'm just a small town girl. And the day of my graduation, Stevie flew us out back to our hometown to where we had our first date and proposed. It was the most magical thing to have happened and although we got soaked because he proposed in the rain, he gave me my very own Delena moment from The Vampire Diaries and I don't think I could ever have loved someone more than I did in that moment.

Stevie even got his record expunged. A couple of years after we left high school; Matilda found out that Brandon was cheating on her with Elle, and got her pregnant. And as retaliation, she went to the police about what happened with Stevie and how they had every intention on having him arrested the night of the school dance. Stevie hadn't actually done anything wrong, but with texts between Brandon and his dad; it actually became clear that twenty-five years earlier, Brandon's dad was the school bully and Stevie's dad, John, was the outcast. And because John married the love of his life and Brandon's Mom left them both, it kind of touched a nerve and history started to repeat itself.

And let's just say, Karma is a bitch! Both Brandon and his dad ended up in jail for the next ten years, and Stevie got a restraining order, and so did Stevie's dad. Matilda only had to

Epilogue

do community service, but her father ended up broke because it turned out he was committing fraud and has ended up in a max security prison, and Elle ended up a single parent to twin boys.

Fast forward two years after our wedding and our little Cindi pops out. Although she was completely unplanned, she made our lives even better than it already was. Her dark brown hair and cute bushy brows means she's the perfect mixture of both Stevie and I and she knows she's loved; she even called me cool once.

And then another two years later, we were blessed with Freddie, named after Freddie Mercury, of course. He is the living breathing double of Stevie and although he is caring, like me, he is more unhinged like Stevie.

I haven't really seen my mom in eight years. That is completely her choice. When she left for that trip before the end of high school, the next time I seen her was court for their divorce. She had met a younger man on her trip, and it turns out she was happier with him than my dad. She tried taking everything from dad during the divorce, but because there was a prenup and she signed it, dad kept the house, and half of his assets because they didn't share any finances, So apart from a couple of hundred dollars, dad didn't have to pay mom anything, even when she pushed for alimony, the courts denied it once they found out that she lived with her new boyfriend and they were actually scheduled to get married in a few months' time once the divorce was final. I think that hurt my dad deeply, but all he said was the guy will realize sooner or later, he will then buy the guy a beer and then send him to therapy. Once we had the kids, she tried being in our life when Freddie was born but turns out all she wanted was a chance at raising another boy, so a restraining order had to be put in place.

Dad has been a great help, he instead started working freelance in his field and after selling the house, he just moved to wherever we moved so he could help with the kids. They love him, and I'm so grateful that I said yes to going out for ice cream all those years ago.

Stevie has taken more of a break these past few months so I can focus on getting my career up and coming, with becoming a parent to two kids so quick, I didn't really have a chance to start my life, I just had to put my dreams on hold. Which I have been totally fine with. However, although Stevie and I love each other dearly, arguments started when there were rumors of yet another tour which meant that I would be left for up to nine months without him, and having to parent two children under ten on my own.

I think once he had time to think about it, he realized how patient I have been, I haven't complained about having to put my dreams on hold, I just did it; without being asked. Sometimes, I did think he expected it from me. But he never said as such.

But a good relationship is built on good communication, and after speaking to each other about our future, he decided to take a step back from the band for a while to let me focus on my dreams of finally publishing my debut novel, Between the Seas. I even published the story under my own name, which meant that Evangeline Lloyd wasn't needed, so I could say goodbye to her so I could start the new chapter in my life. Publicly, I'm known as Jolie Mason, but legally, I'm Jolie Pritchard and took that name happily.

The story follows Daniel and India and their love story

Epilogue

from two different parts of the world and how they came together. Although by the time it was published it had changed dramatically, it was still picked up by a publisher and within a year it was published and on the shelves in the likes of Barnes and Noble and Books-A-Million.

Stevie was so proud, he still is. He constantly posts it to his story or on a grid post on his Instagram, with the hashtag #proudhusband.

The book became a international success, and before I knew it, talks of a book tour, merchandise and possibly a sequel were in the mix. All the things that I had dreamed of when I was younger. Stevie pushed for it all, but I decided for a very small book tour in America for now. I'm still quite shy in person and if I did something as big as a international book tour, I knew I would get overwhelmed and awkward. But one day I'll do it. Once Cindi and Freddie are older, maybe.

After a few more complaints and moans from myself, we head downstairs as a family to begin to start our day. It's barely ten o'clock, yet I feel absolutely drained like I have fought with my kids all day already. But that's the whole point of being a parent, you always wake up exhausted.

"Pancakes or waffles?" I ask them as we approach the kitchen.

"Both!" Stevie screams in excitement, and both of the kids shout in agreement.

"Ignore Dad," I say to our children. "Pancakes or waffles?" I repeat.

"Pancakes!" They shout in unison before running through to their playroom down the hall. I look to Stevie with a grin as although he is the biggest kid out of the three of them, he also forgets that I'm the boss in the house, he's just the boss in the bedroom.

Dealing With The Outcast

"How is it that you can get them to listen, but I can't?" He whines as he approaches me at the counter. "You're so much better at this than I am."

He looks down, yet I am quick to raise his head to look at me. "We do this together remember. Besides," I say moving away slightly. "They hate waffles."

"I should know that." he says under his breath. "I feel like I've missed out on so much." He exhales. "They don't hate me, do they?" He asks suddenly and I feel my heart ache.

"They could never hate you; they love you. They just see you as the cool dad, that's all." I smile at him. "You've wasted no time, there is still plenty of time to raise them together and for us to learn every new thing about them."

He smiles at me reassuringly. "This is why I love you," He explains cupping my face and giving me a kiss. "You always know what to say."

I look up at him through my eyelashes. "Well, yeah!" I say sarcastically. "I'm super Mom."

I watch Stevie cringe in horror. "True, but never say that out loud again. I've just felt myself die inside."

"Stop being dramatic," I laugh slightly pushing him away. "I'm just pleased you agree."

He smiles to me, "Of course I agree."

"Good." I say, leaning over and giving him a kiss, which he seems told hold just that little bit too long. "Don't start." I warn him as I go to walk away but he reaches for my waist, pulling me in closer.

"Start what?" He asks playfully, kissing me again just a little bit longer.

"You know what." I remind him, while trying (barely) to get out of his grip.

Epilogue

"I have no idea what you're talking about, kinky."

"Sure, you do. Your seductive kisses are the reason I'm pregnant again." I blurt out without thinking. *Shit.*

He steps back from me, a mixture of confusion and happiness on his face as he tries to understand what I have just said. "What?"

"I found out yesterday." I smile at him, before opening the drawer in front of me to show him a pregnancy test with two very distinctive lines. "But I wanted to tell you better than this!" I exclaim, annoyed at myself for ruining it.

"Shut it, kinky." he says, staring at the test in disbelief.

"You're not mad?" I ask him and he looks to me, tears in his eyes and a smile plastered all over his face.

"Mad?" he asks almost in horror. "This is the best news!" He exclaims, picking me up and spinning me around the kitchen. Giggles and happiness fill the air as we soak up the feeling together. Another little monster, as Stevie calls them. "I love you." He says once he places me down to look at him. "Ah... I love you; I love you, I love you!" he exclaims, giving me a long, deep and passionate kiss.

"I'm excited."

"Me too." I watch as the imaginary clogs begin to turn in his brain.

"Don't even think about it."

"Can we name this one Prince?"

"Fuck off, Stevie."

THE END

Afterword

So many people to thank, oh my goodness!

When I first thought about Jolie and Stevie's story. It wasn't anything that it is today. Originally it was going to be something along the lines of the cheerleader and the rock star, but when I had the idea for Jolie, she didn't match up to what I was thinking in my head, or what I was originally drafting. She was quiet, reserved, her very own version of a freak. When I decided to make her a smutty book writer, everything began to fall into place, and the story, although it has changed since it's original draft, was something that I ended up loving even more.

Stevie on the other hand, I wanted someone who I could relate to. Like a lot of the characters I create, I always want to create someone who I know I would want to be friends with if I was ever given the option. Stevie's music taste is the perfect mixture of my Mam's with Bon Jovi, and The Police, for my late dad. I always wanted him to have the kindheartedness of my late Grandad Norman, who, if it wasn't for his relentless nagging to get me to read, I wouldn't have my novels today.

My sister was the whole inspiration for Stevie's chaos. And I

Afterword

couldn't love her more because of it.

To the rest of my family, who buy every book, who post anything I post about my books.

To my friends who stick by me, who help me off the ledge when I'm losing my rag about a story or a character, this is to you!

To Joseph, who puts up with my stress when it's deadline day and he's trying to distract me with Tiktok's to get me to take a break. Little does he know, that's why I'm distracted all the time leading up to deadline day.

To Hayley, fucking hell Hayley!!!! Who created the most beautiful cover to represent Stevie and Jolie and their story. I love you. Thank you.

To my troublemakers who stuck by me and waited that little bit extra while I finally got my mental health in check to be able to start and finish their story.

And lastly to you my dear reader, for spending your time reading my story about two completely different people who ended up together. I loved Jolie and Stevie's story from the minute I started. Although it's small, it tells the story I wanted.

I love you. And thank you!!!!!

About the Author

Torrie Jones is a indie author based in Newcastle upon Tyne, England, UK. Growing up surrounded by shows such as NCIS, Criminal Minds and Rizzoli & Isles, she wanted her stories to show something she is passionate about, solving crimes.

She is a content creator, nerd and animal lover who has a dog named Penny and cat named Sheldon.

Whilst most people have kids, Torrie talks about her characters as if they were her children. She loves each one individually, apart from the ones who have ended up on the naughty step.

She published her debut novel The Lies We Tell back in May of 2022, and has not only continued that series, but gone on to tell other stories of some new and old characters.

To keep up with all of the gossip, make sure to follow Torrie on Instagram, like her Facebook page and her Tiktok's. All updates will be on there and her website www.torriemaryjones.com.

You can connect with me on:

🌐 https://www.torriemaryjones.com

📘 https://www.facebook.com/groups/troublebookclub/?mibextid=oMANbw

📷 https://www.instagram.com/torriejonesauthor

Also by Torrie Jones

The Hidden Jules Series:
  The Lies We Tell
  The Secrets We Keep
  The Betrayal That Follows
  The Hidden Jules Series - Book 4 (September 27th 2024)
  The Hidden Jules Series - Book 5 (June 6th 2025)

The Troubled Series:
  Hate you too
  Loathe you entirely (February 14th 2024)
  The Troubled Series - Book 3 (February 14th 2025)

Secret Project:
  Unnamed (December 31st 2025)

Printed in Great Britain
by Amazon